# Hot Springs Murder

*Jackson Hole Moose's Bakery Not So Cozy Mystery #2*

Sue Pepper

DIMICK LANE
PRESS

This is a work of fiction. Names, characters, places, and incidents are the product of the author's imagination or are used fictitiously, and any resemblance to actual persons, living or dead, business establishments, events, or locales is entirely coincidental.

Copyright © 2022 Sue Pepper

All rights reserved.

No part of this book may be reproduced, stored in a retrieval system, or transmitted in any forms, or by any means, electronic, mechanical, photocopying, recording, or otherwise, without prior written permission of the author. Trademarked names appear throughout this book. Rather than use a trademark symbol with every occurrence of a trademarked name, names are used in an editorial fashion, with no intention of infringement of the respective owner's trademark(s).

Print ISBN: 979-8-9856200-1-6

Published by Dimick Lane Press

Cover Design by Sue Pepper

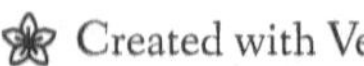 Created with Vellum

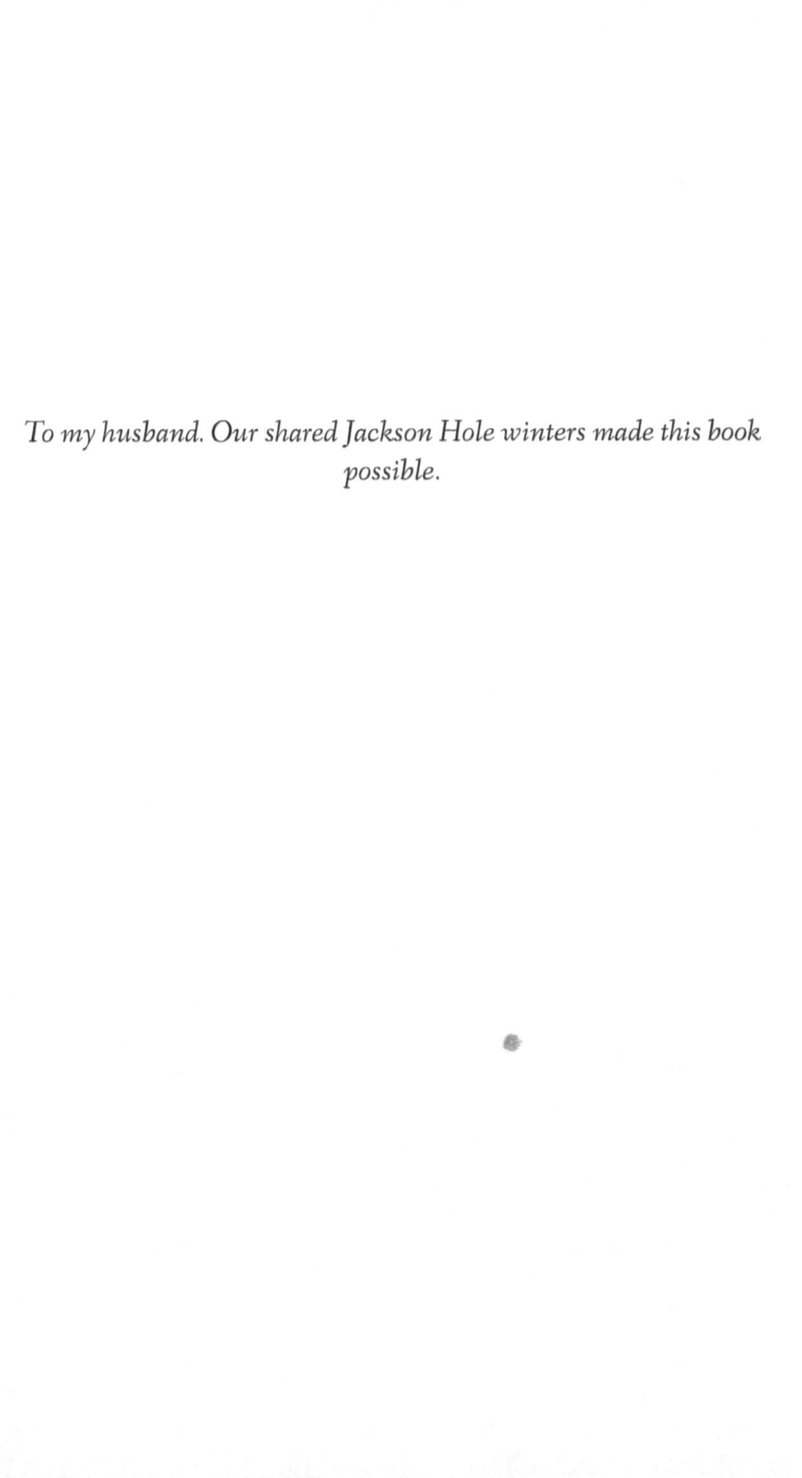

*To my husband. Our shared Jackson Hole winters made this book possible.*

# Chapter One

The morning was cold, the coffee was hot, the line was long, and Sadie Moose could see her profit-and-loss statement edging into the black in her head.

"Right behind you, boss!" Kendall Craig, Sadie's head barista and terrifyingly efficient Gen Z friend, said, slipping behind her with an armload of paper-wrapped baked goods. "They can't get enough of these carrot cake muffins today."

"Good," Sadie said with a satisfied smile. "I intended them to be irresistible." She opened the window on her side of the just-opened Moose's Bakery Hoback Junction Coffee Kiosk and stuck her head out to greet the next customer, a dark-haired woman in a red puffy coat with bags under her eyes and a toddler yelling in the backseat.

"Vanilla latte with a double shot please," the woman said over her shoulder, craning around to placate the toddler with a bag of crackers.

Sadie turned towards her newly installed espresso machine, Francesca. The sleek, Italian-made system was sister to Luciana, Sadie's beloved machine installed at her bakery in Jackson Hole, twenty minutes down the highway. Her hands flew over

Francesca in practiced moves, dispensing fresh ground beans into the portafilter and inserting it into the brew group. She pressed the buttons for a double shot.

Sadie foamed the milk for the tired mom's latte and poured it in, topping the cup with a lid and sliding it into a cardboard sleeve. She added the final touch—a cinnamon moose candy, like a cinnamon bear but more on brand—to the lid and handed it over. The woman held up her phone for Sadie to scan for payment, and was on her way, the screaming from the backseat quelled. The next car pulled up. Hot dang! It was 7:30 a.m. and her line was five cars deep. Sadie took the next vehicle's order, but before she could start it, Kendall stopped her.

"Hand me that cuppie-on-a-stickie, boss. I'll switch sides with ya," she said. "That customer's for you." The kiosk, a 250-square-foot shed with sliding windows on both sides, accommodated two lines to speed caffeine delivery.

"Oh?" Sadie asked, handing Kendall the portafilter she'd just filled with grounds and glancing out the window.

"It's your boyfriend," Kendall said in a mock whisper, winking at her, and Sadie laughed, pushing past her.

Sadie felt a flutter in her stomach. Boyfriend was a loaded word for what the man outside her kiosk window was. They were having fun. Keeping it light. Sadie ran a pale white hand over her ponytail, her long brown hair pulled back, and made a mental note to add a small mirror above the hand washing sink. Did she have mascara smeared around her eyes? She seemed to always have mascara smeared around her eyes.

Sadie opened the window, letting in an arctic blast of frigid January air. She smiled at the tanned, dark-haired man in the older Ford pickup who was smiling back at her, his white teeth a flash in his close-cropped dark beard. He slipped his sunglasses off, revealing tired dark blue eyes with crinkles around the corners that proved he was usually smiling.

"Hey," Jake Moreno said.

"Hey," Sadie replied.

"Hey!" Kendall yelled from the other side of the kiosk. Sadie rolled her eyes. Her staff constantly made the same jokes.

"Headed home?" Sadie asked. There were no other cars behind Jake in the southbound lane, most cars heading into Jackson preferring to use the northbound window for ease of zipping on and off the highway.

"Yep," Jake said, yawning. "No coffee. I'm beat and need sleep, but maybe a muffin?"

"You got it." Sadie turned to the display of baked goods, bagging a giant carrot cake muffin for him. "On the house," she winked, passing it out the window.

"You're the best, Sadie Moose."

"Aww," Sadie blushed.

Jake leaned closer and Sadie leaned out of the window towards him, and he brushed a kiss over her mouth. Just a light passing of the lips. They were cold, and hers were too. It was in the teens and the weather report said it wasn't climbing above freezing today. Their air puffed together as they pulled apart, both smiling. A car that had pulled in behind Jake honked and Sadie waved at them, laughing.

"Sleep well," Sadie said, pulling away. "Call me later?"

"Yeah." Jake glanced in his rearview mirror. "I will. Hey, want to go to Pritchard Hot Springs with me in the groomer tonight? I only have one road to do, and the caretaker said he'd keep the springs open for me if I wanted to soak when I was done."

Jake was a wildland firefighter for the United States Forest Service, wearing the green pants and yellow shirt uniform of those that fought fire in the forests and wildlands, not in structures. He worked nine months out of the year, and was laid off for three. Since he lived in employer-provided housing, his boss found work for him throughout the winter so he could continue to pay rent. This year, he was grooming snowmobile and cross-country ski trails across the Forest. He worked at night, when everyone was off the trails.

Sadie considered his offer. It was Friday, and she had nothing else scheduled. It would be a cold, moonlit January night. Perfect for a soak in the hot springs.

"You could stay at my place after?"

Sadie's stomach did that flutter again. She and Jake had dated before, for about six months, before he'd been forced to leave the valley after his housing had become untenable. He'd been back since December, having accepted a promotion on the Bridger Hotshots that offered permanent housing. For at least three years, at which point he had to move out. He lived at the base of the trail that led to Pritchard Hot Springs, one of the many hot springs scattered throughout the Tetons.

"I'd love that," Sadie said finally, committing. "If Tyrone can hang at your house while we're gone?" She was sure Kendall or her roommate Kamari Robinson, another of Sadie's baristas, could let her chocolate lab, Tyrone, named after the Backyardigans moose, in and out and feed him overnight. But Sadie hated to spend the night away from him. KitKat, as friends of the two called them, lived in Sadie's basement apartment as part of their compensation and were frequent Tyrone-sitters.

"I'd be sad if he didn't come. It's a date." Jake winked at her and then handed her a five-dollar bill. "For that poor person behind me, yeah?"

"You bet." Sadie blew a kiss as he drove away, and then took the order of the annoyed man in the car behind him. The pinched look on his face eased when Sadie told him Jake paid for his coffee, and she'd thrown in a muffin no charge.

Kendall and Sadie worked wordlessly through the next rush, dancing around each other in a well-coordinated ballet of efficiency. Kendall was in charge of the music, and this morning they were jamming to Norwegian death metal. It was a vibe. They'd been working in the kiosk together for the last week since the grand opening, and they'd worked out the kinks. Sadie was interviewing potential baristas Monday in hopes she could train them and transition back into supervision only within the month.

During a lull, Kendall and Sadie gulped water and stood under the wall-mounted heater, warming their hands. Kendall swept her warmed palms through her close-cropped brown hair and yawned hugely, scrunching up her freckled nose.

"So..." she eyed Sadie. "First overnight on this back-on-again cycle, hmmm?"

Sadie's cheeks reddened. "We're just having fun, Kendall."

"Right. Fun. On your romantic date to picturesque hot springs under the full moon followed by warming each other in his bed."

Sadie pictured the scene. Her cheeks got redder, but there was a heat in her belly. She'd had her heart broken by her childhood crush, Merritt West, last October. The circumstances that had pulled them together—namely finding the dead body of Merritt's ex-girlfriend and Sadie's lifelong tormenter, then being named as suspects before they stumbled upon the real killer and almost died—had been intense, and their brief affair had been, too. But Merritt had a job that meant he couldn't stay, and Sadie wouldn't leave the valley, so they didn't have a future together.

Sadie had moped through Thanksgiving. Then Jake had shown up at the bakery staff holiday night out, and he'd been a tall, hard-bodied, handsome port in the storm. Familiar, but not recently familiar. Always smiling, always happy, and an excellent kisser, Jake Moreno had been the perfect balm for her heartache. They'd been going out a couple times a week since, but they hadn't advanced to overnights. It was almost silly.

They'd been together before. But it still felt like the first time all over again.

"Yeah, it's pretty hot," Sadie admitted, waving at the car that had pulled up to the northbound window. "But we're just having fun. I'm too young to settle down."

"You're thirty-two, Moose."

"Yep. Far too young." Sadie winked at her.

"I'll always prefer 007, anyway," Kendall sighed. Merritt had a job with the State Department he couldn't talk about, spent a lot of time traveling, and was known to carry a firearm and have friends in high places. Kendall thought he was the best. It might have been love, except Kendall liked girls.

Sadie smiled sadly. "Like Jack Reacher, he was here, he did the job, and then he left, my friend."

Sadie opened the window to greet her customer, leaving Kendall muttering behind her, but the woman in the seat wasn't looking at Sadie. She was craning her neck to see something in the parking lot. Sadie peered over her car and gasped, startled. A brawl was unfolding just feet away.

# Chapter Two

The coffee kiosk was in the Junction Market parking lot, close to the highway with an easy entrance and exit. Closer to the market, several men pushed and shoved one another. Sadie saw puffs of air and heard their muffled shouts. As she watched, a tall, wiry man got a good punch in on a shorter, rounder man. The third man tried to break them apart. A small crowd had formed at the market entrance, but Sadie couldn't tell if they were going to intervene or just watch curiously.

"Yikes," Sadie said, and the woman in the car, a redhead with her hair up in a wild topknot, turned to look at her with wide eyes.

"Should we call someone?" The woman asked, her voice strained.

"Uh...maybe?"

"What's happening?" Kendall said behind Sadie. "Oh, wow. Get him!"

"Kendall, you don't even know who those people are."

"Not true. The one taking a beating is Royce Hensley, the housing manager for the Forest Service. That guy's a dick."

Sadie made a face. She knew that guy, too. Good-natured Jake, who got along with everyone, had been complaining about him last week. He wasn't a landlord, more like the maintenance guy, but he acted like the mayor of the housing complex and expected everyone to treat him as such.

"Still," Sadie murmured.

"I'm calling someone," the redhead said, snatching her phone from her center console. She frowned at it. "No signal."

"Right." The high walls of the Snake River Canyon blocked most cell phone signals at the Junction, but Sadie had Wi-Fi at the kiosk that let her employees call out if needed. "Kendall, call the sheriff. I'm going over there."

"I should come with you, boss," Kendall said, puffing up. Kendall was a raft guide and ski patroller. Though petite in stature, she was built.

"I'm not going to get involved," Sadie promised. "I'll take my phone in case I need to film something."

Kendall was talking into her phone now, reporting the skirmish to the 911 dispatcher. Sadie looked at her customer, who was back to watching the unfolding scene with rapt attention. "Kendall will get you a coffee once she's off the phone," Sadie promised.

The woman nodded distractedly, and Sadie moved to the back door to slip her puffy coat over her vest and slide her fingers into gloves. She pulled on a knit hat, her high ponytail distorting it, but she didn't have time to worry about that. Sadie opened the backdoor to the kiosk and gingerly made her way down the steps. She'd put down de-icer earlier, but winter ice and snow had built up a dangerous slick around the exit. Bracing herself to the cold, Sadie hurried across the parking lot until she could hear the words being shouted.

The attacker, the tall wiry man, was being held back by the third man now, but he and Royce were still shouting at each other. Royce, a sour-faced white man in his mid-fifties in a red stocking cap, had a cut under his right eye and kept rubbing blood away from it.

"Attacking your superior! You're going to lose your job and your housing now, you moron!" Royce shouted.

"You're not my superior, you asshole!" the other man yelled, fighting against the brawny man holding him.

Royce sneered at him but said nothing. He looked around shiftily, like he was thinking of running.

"It wasn't your business! You're always sticking your nose into everyone's business! I could lose my housing because of you!" the man shouted. Sadie took a minute to get a good look at him. He was a white man with ruddy cheeks and a salt and pepper scruff. Sadie guessed he was around the same age as Royce.

"That's where you always get it wrong, Jerry." Royce was holding a handkerchief to his eye now, but Sadie could still see the mean glint there. "Everything that happens at Poplar is my business."

Jerry made a strangled sound and pulled out of the arms of the man who was holding him back, lunging for Royce. Royce took a step to run, but Jerry crashed into him and they fell to the ground. Their arms wheeled as they tried to land blows on each other. Sadie glanced at the man who had been holding Jerry and suddenly recognized him.

"Cole," Sadie said. "Do something!" Cole Richards, Jake's neighbor, a fellow crew member on Jake's hotshot crew, looked at her, his face blank. He was a white man in his mid-thirties, his brown hair standing up wildly as if his knit cap had been knocked askew in the scuffle.

"I tried, Sadie." He smoothed his hair and put his hands in the pockets of his Carhartt coat resolutely. "But Royce deserves this."

Sadie gaped at him. Sadie didn't know Cole well, but from her interactions with him since she'd started hanging around with Jake, he seemed like a kind man. He had a gorgeous wife and a two-year-old he often took out on a sled, pulling her around the housing complex, gently pushing her down inclines while she squealed happily. What had Royce done that Cole thought he'd earned the beating Jerry was giving him?

In the distance, sirens wailed. Cole glanced around but stood firm, watching the two men rolling around in the icy parking lot. They were both exhausted, gasping for air and grappling with one another.

"My business," Jerry kept grunting as he attempted to land a punch on Royce's kidneys.

Sadie glanced back at the coffee kiosk. A line of cars had formed again, but the red-headed woman's car was still parked in front of the window. She and Kendall both watched the scene, as did everyone else in line, Sadie realized. Plenty of witnesses to this attack. Jerry was going to be in a lot of trouble.

Finally, a Teton County Sheriff's Office truck pulled into the lot and came squealing to a stop a few feet away. Sadie backed up as the deputy jumped out of the car and ran at the two men grappling on the ground, pulling at Jerry's shoulders.

Another vehicle, this one a white and green SUV with the Forest Service shield on the door and LEO 3 painted on the side, roared up next to them. A tall, olive-skinned woman with her long black hair pulled back in a French braid hopped out. She took one look at the two men on the ground and stiffened. Instead of moving to assist the deputy, she bustled closer, then yelled.

"Jerry Givens and Royce Hensley, stop this right now or I'm calling the Ranger!"

The two men froze. Jerry rolled off Royce and laid on the ground, panting. There was blood on his face, but Sadie couldn't tell if it was his or Royce's. Purple bruising bloomed on his cheek. The deputy moved between the men as the woman planted her hands on her hips and scowled at them.

"You're supposed to be pillars of this community and I'm called in to a fistfight in the market parking lot and it's you two? You'll be lucky if you're both not fired."

The men had the decency to look chagrined.

"When you're done scolding them, can you help me cuff them?" The deputy asked wryly, and Sadie had to stifle a giggle. The woman, who Sadie recognized as another neighbor of Jake's, had a way about her that made Sadie feel like she should apologize, even though she wasn't involved.

"They can cuff themselves for all I care," the woman frowned. "Especially you, Royce. You're a reserve deputy. The Sheriff will take your badge if you're responsible for this." She glanced around, spotted Sadie, then walked towards her. The deputy was giving Royce a hard time behind her, but she paid him no mind.

"Did you see who started it?" She asked Sadie, her voice brusque.

"I didn't," Sadie said. "I was over in the coffee kiosk." She gestured that direction.

The woman took in the kiosk, then looked back at Sadie, sticking out her hand. "I'm Officer Elaina Hernandez."

"Sadie Moose."

"You look familiar."

"I'm dating Jake Moreno. I think I've seen you around Poplar." The housing complex, a hodgepodge of trailer homes, old stick-built homes, and tiny homes, was in the river bottom of the canyon along the Snake River. Cottonwood and poplar trees kept it hidden from the nearby highway. The complex had an official name, but everyone called it Poplar.

"Oh yeah," Officer Hernandez said, her voice warming. "I remember seeing you around. You own Moose's?"

"I do." Sadie's eyes flitted to the scene playing out behind her. Both men had sat up and been handcuffed by the deputy. They looked sheepish. Cole had disappeared.

"It's great that you took over the coffee stand. I'll stop by soon."

"We open at six," Sadie said. "Your first coffee's on me."

"Great. So you didn't see who started it. What were they saying to each other?"

Sadie chose her words carefully. She recounted Royce's insistence on being Jerry's boss and what Jerry did being his business. She described how Royce had taunted Jerry into attacking him again, and the threat he'd leveled at Jerry, that he'd lose both his job and his housing.

"I take it Jerry is another neighbor?"

Officer Hernandez nodded, but said nothing more. Another sheriff's deputy had arrived on the scene, and she waved at him. "Give me your number, and me or one of these county knuckleheads will find you later for an official witness statement. I'm going to go help these deputies with these two. Then I'm going to have to call the Ranger. You've got a line forming." She nodded at the coffee kiosk and Sadie turned. She could see Kendall's hands flying over Francesca as she tried to keep up.

"Sounds good, thanks Officer Hernandez."

"Elaina," she corrected.

"Thanks Elaina."

Sadie headed back to the coffee kiosk, her mind whirling. She hadn't seen a fight since several summers ago when two drunk tourists had fought over whether it was okay to pet the stuffed bison outside the mercantile on town square. That had ended with them both in the back of a police car with I ♥ Jackson Hole hats on their heads given to them by the store's owner, who'd seen a happy boost in business because of the extra attention.

This was Jackson Hole, where 11,000 locals, a few dozen billionaire absent second homeowners, and three million tourists a year mingled in a narrow valley in the shadow of the cathedral peaks of the Tetons. Locals fought to survive here, cramming roommates into studio apartments, sleeping in their cars on forest roads, persisting while their names slogged up the list to be eligible to buy affordable housing that could guarantee their permanence in the valley. It was a grind, one the wealthy that called Jackson Hole their playground often refused to see.

If Royce had jeopardized Jerry's housing, Sadie could understand why Jerry was so upset. From what Sadie had heard about Royce, he wasn't a nice man. Sadie hoped Jerry wouldn't get in too much trouble. But as she stepped into the coffee kiosk, she saw the first sheriff's deputy was helping him into the backseat of his truck, and her stomach dropped. Assault was assault. It looked like Jerry would pay for what he'd done.

# Chapter Three

Officer Hernandez, or Elaina, as she'd insisted on being called, came by the bakery while Sadie was prepping the next day's doughs for her assistant bakers. Elaina had coffee—black, one sugar—and a croissant while she took Sadie's meager statement. According to Elaina, Jerry had been charged with assault, but was out on bail. Sadie locked up the bakery at six o'clock, went home, showered, ate a quick dinner, and packed an overnight bag for her and Tyrone.

She left Jackson, Tyrone riding in the back of her Subaru, around eight o'clock. They drove through town, then South Jackson, then along the Snake River, where the narrow road offered glimpses of the river below. She drove past the dark coffee kiosk and the quiet parking lot where she'd seen the fight earlier, then around the roundabout at the junction, continuing south through the Snake River Canyon.

As she drove into the small community, she expected to see evidence of the neighborhood tribulations on display, but saw only the normal smoke billowing out of chimneys, warmly lit windows, and piles of snow. There was two feet on the ground and more in the piles, and they weren't through the snowiest months yet.

Jake greeted her at the door with a kiss, and then they got Tyrone acquainted with the dog bed Jake had bought for him.

"What do you know about Jerry and Royce?" She asked, feeding Tyrone a treat as she petted his soft ears.

Jake grimaced. "I saw Royce walking around with a heck of a shiner earlier, but I don't know what the fight was about. Everyone's staying in their houses, waiting for it to blow over." He handed her a filled water bowl for Tyrone, then turned back to fill a bag with snacks and thermoses. "Probably deserved it though, the bastard," he said under his breath.

Tyrone settled, they piled into Jake's truck and drove the short distance to the area where the road was closed for the winter.

Outfitters ran winter tours to the hot springs, and everyone was coming back from their day trips as Jake and Sadie prepared to depart. The lot was full of trucks and snowmobile trailers and even a dogsledder's rig, a truck with a multi-doored kennel on the back capable of carrying a dozen dogs. Sharp barks filled the air as dogs loaded in. The hot springs closed at six, and it was an hour's snowmobile ride, or a longer dog sled ride, on the groomed trail.

It was a cold, brilliantly clear night, moonlight illuminating the snowy world around them. The groomer, a large red tractor-looking machine on tracks with an enclosed cab, was loud, so Sadie and Jake couldn't talk much on the way. They satisfied themselves with occasional shouts to point something out and small smiles at one another. The defrost was on full blast so Jake could see out the windows. He occasionally had to open his side window to look out and check the pattern the groomer was leaving on the snow, so it was freezing in the cab. Jake had warned Sadie, though, so she had dressed for the cold in fleece-lined base layers, snow bibs, snow boots, and her ski jacket. Underneath it all was a red bikini.

As they made their way slowly in the groomer, the machine left straight tracks behind it, smoothing out snowmobile ruts, skier tracks, and dog footprints and pushing the snow into flat, easily crossable terrain. They passed a few snowmobilers as they motored up, and Jake commented he thought one of them was Cole. Sadie wanted to ask Jake about Cole's insistence that Royce deserved the beating he got today, but she couldn't talk to him over the loud noise of the groomer.

Mostly, though, it was just them working their way up the mountain trail. In the summer, it was an actual road, but the Forest maintained it for snowmobiles and skiers only in the winter. A creek ran next to the road, covered now in ice and snow. The moon dramatized everything, and Sadie could see what she thought were all the stars visible to a human in the sky. The moon hung large and full, casting the snow-covered trees in a blueish glow. It was peaceful, and Sadie understood why Jake liked this job. It was a pleasant break from the rigors of wildland fire, when he worked sixteen-hour days doing the grueling, back-breaking work of line digging, sawing, and clearing brush ahead of fires across the west.

"Moose!" Jake shouted, and Sadie swung her head around to look at him, but he laughed and pointed out the window, bringing the groomer to a stop. Sadie followed his finger and grinned. A large bull moose, still wearing his large paddles, stood in the creek bed. He turned to look at them, and Sadie imagined she could see his large dark eyes, so like the large dark eyes of her chocolate lab. They sat for a few minutes, watching each other. Then the moose turned away, snuffling around the base of a snow-laden spruce tree for something edible, forgetting the red machine and its inhabitants.

Sadie smiled the rest of the way to the hot springs. She

thought of the moose, and of her moosey dog, and how happy she was to be a Moose that owned a bakery called Moose's in a town known for its moose population.

The creek thawed and steam rose above it as they rounded a bend and took a right fork onto the hot springs road. A few more turns on the narrow track and they emerged in a large parking area. Snow had been scraped into a towering pile on one side of the lot. There was a small tracked UTV parked near the caretaker's cottage, lights shining out onto the snow, smoke curling out of the chimney, and one snowmobile parked. Otherwise, the parking lot was empty, as expected. Jake frowned at the one snowmobile as he parked the groomer. He cut the engine, and Sadie's ears roared in the silence.

"Not expecting that one?" Her voice was louder than she meant it to be in the sudden quiet.

"Nope," Jake said. He opened the cab door, grabbing the bag he'd packed for them and the bag she'd brought with a change of clothes. "I'll come over to help you with the door."

*Such chivalry.*

He opened the door for her and held out a gloved hand to help her on the slippery step, onto the track, and onto the ground. The frigid air bit her cheeks. It was colder up here at a higher elevation, easily in the single digits. Sadie sniffed. Her nostrils didn't freeze together, so she knew it was above freezing. The air was still, at least. Any breeze would've made it too bitter to soak. Sadie shivered in anticipation of the warm water. Jake grinned at her, moonlight casting a wicked shadow on it, and Sadie shivered again, this time in anticipation of being in the hot springs with Jake. He closed up the groomer, and they started toward the path to the springs.

Jake stopped at the parked snowmobile, a frown appearing again.

"Probably broke down," he said, looking at her, face clearing. "I bet they come up tomorrow to get it."

That sounded reasonable to Sadie. They set off on the snow-covered path, walking in the open for a moment before they moved into the trees. They crossed a wooden bridge, the snow packed by many boots, the creek burbling beneath them, and turned a bend, and then the pool was in sight. The Civilian Conservation Corps had contained the natural hot spring into a concrete pool in the 1930s. A rough wooden fence surrounded it, steam wafting into the sky. Inside the fence was a weathered shack with rustic bathrooms and changing rooms. There was a combo lock on the gate, and Jake took off a glove to enter the combination, then gestured for her to enter before him.

It was a picturesque sight, and a rare one. To see the hot springs after closing in the dark on a moonlit night was something few people got to see. The oval pool backed up against natural rocks that cascaded down the hillside. The largest of the rocks were part of the pool itself and attracted bikini-clad sunbathers in the summer, including Sadie in her teen years. A wooden boardwalk, kept mostly snow and ice-free thanks to the heat of the water and the work of the caretaker, surrounded the half of the pool that wasn't up against the hillside. With the snow on the rocks, the moon low in the sky, and the steam rising from the water, it was unlike anything Sadie had ever seen. She turned to Jake as he closed the gate and wrapped her arms around him. "Thank you so much for bringing me here. This is amazing."

Jake squeezed her and brushed a kiss on her chilled cheek. "Let's get you in before you freeze."

"I hope that water's warm," Sadie grimaced.

"Me too. Don't want to turn you into a popsicle."

"I'd be a cute one at least."

"And a tasty one, I bet," Jake growled, nipping at her neck before pushing her towards the changing rooms.

They were chilly but clean. Amos, the caretaker Jake had mentioned, must have cleaned them once the hot springs closed. Sadie took off her layers carefully, using the hooks in the changing room to make sure everything would stay dry. By the time she stripped to her bikini and socks, she was shivering. She left on her hat and then pulled off her socks and slipped into the flip-flops she'd brought. She looked around for a mirror, but there wasn't one.

*Second time today I have no idea what I look like,* she thought. She'd taken off her makeup when she showered after work, so she knew there wasn't mascara around her eyes or flour in her hair at least, but oh well. She glanced down at her bikini. The swimsuit showed off her assets. The vintage-inspired cup bra pushed her breasts up and out and the high-waisted bottom smoothed her rolls into voluptuous curves. *Bombshell,* she thought to herself, grinning.

Bracing herself for the cold, she took a deep breath and walked out the door.

* * *

If Sadie was a bombshell, Jake was an ad from an outdoor catalog. She found him waiting for her at the steps to enter the pool. He wore the same green stocking cap he'd worn up, a pair of vintage blue Patagonia baggies shorts that had seen better days, and a grin. She didn't stop herself from ogling him. He was tall with a working man's muscles, strength that was built swinging a Pulaski, not in the gym. He had a light dusting of dark hair across his tanned chest, which showed power, but no high maintenance abs. And he was looking at her, all round five feet, almost five inches of her, with hunger in his eyes.

"Look at you, sexy thing," he growled, reaching out a hand to grab hers and pull her towards him. He ran his large palms along her arms to her waist, pulling her in for a kiss. It was a long moment before he pulled away. "You're going to freeze, though, time to get in."

A light breeze had picked up while they were wrapped in each other, and Sadie's body was covered in goosebumps. She turned to the pool to step in, grabbing the handrail to steady herself. The water was completely invisible in the steam coming off of it. She put one foot in, but then stopped.

"What?" Jake asked.

"I...I thought I saw something in the water."

"What, a shark?" His voice was teasing, but the hand on the small of her back was comforting.

Sadie peered into the mist. Was that a swimsuit?

"No..." Sadie trailed off. The breeze picked up again, clearing the mist momentarily, and the next sound she made was a scream.

# Chapter Four

Jake splashed into the water, pulling at what Sadie had thought was just an errant swimsuit floating in the water, but was actually a fully clothed body. He rolled the body over, shouting, but didn't pull the person out, something he saw making him stop. Instead, he hustled back up the steps, pulling Sadie, shaking and whimpering from cold and shock, off the pool deck and into the changing rooms.

"Wrap yourself up," he ordered, his own voice shaky but firm. He pulled a fluffy towel out of her bag and pushed it at her. "Put on clothes when you can. I'm going to get Amos to radio for help."

"Is...it...?"

Jake's face was grim, his normally upturned lips in a hard, flat line.

"It's a man, and he's dead."

"Oh my God."

Jake wrapped the towel around her. He gripped her shoulders. "Stay in here. Lock the door behind me. Don't open it for anyone but me."

Sadie barely heard the words, but when they broke through her shocked brain, a stab of fear cut through her.

"Right. Okay." She took a deep breath, remembering the breathing exercises her best friend and meditation coach Paige Gates-Ortiz had taught her, and then took another one. Jake was staring at her worriedly. "I'm okay," she reassured him, putting a hand on his chest and meeting his eyes. "I'll lock the door. Watch your back."

Jake was reluctant, but he left her, opening the door and looking out before ducking out and into his own changing room. After a few moments, she heard him go back by her changing room door, his boot sounds heavy on the wooden boardwalk. Too soon, his footfalls were silenced on the snow-covered path, and Sadie was utterly alone, just her and a dead body in the hot springs.

She shivered again. The towel wasn't doing much to warm her. She hung it on a hook and hastily dressed, layering base layers, then mid-layers, then snow clothes over the bikini, letting the movements calm her mind. She didn't let her brain remember the last time she'd stumbled across a dead body. Or at least, she hadn't let her brain think of the last time she'd stumbled across a dead body, until right then. Sadie felt queasy as she sat, fully dressed and warming up, on a narrow wooden bench along the back wall of the room. That experience, last October, had almost taken Sadie's life, and she'd never wanted to get involved in another mystery again. And yet, here she was.

Sadie thought of what she'd seen in the pool. Jake had told her it was a man, and that he was dead. She had gotten only the impression of snow clothes, a reflective strip on the legs of the pants that someone would wear if they were snowmobiling. Perhaps this was just a terrible accident? Someone had been left behind by their group somehow, and had tripped or slipped, hit their head, and fell in and drowned? Maybe they'd been up here on their own. But Amos had cleaned the changing rooms between when the pool closed and when they'd arrived. Wouldn't he have seen someone in the water? And the gate had been locked. What did that mean?

Time passed as Sadie considered these things. Slowly, she stopped shaking. She stayed in tune to every sound around her, hoping to hear Jake coming back, and hoping she didn't hear anyone else creeping around. She didn't have a watch and had left her phone, which had no service, in the groomer. How long had she been alone? Should she go after Jake? She would feel more comfortable in the cab of the locked groomer instead of in this small, dim room. Sadie recognized she was panicking and did her box breathing. *Breathe in for a count of four, hold it for four, breathe out for four, hold it for four, repeat.*

She was repeating those steps in her head and breathing steadily when Jake returned, a tentative knock at the door and a, "Sadie, let me in," signaling his arrival.

Sadie stood and opened the door a crack, making sure it was just Jake and not Jake and anyone else, and then let him in.

"Amos is wasted," Jake said with disgust. "I had to pound on the door for five minutes to wake him. I thought something had happened to him too, but he finally came to the door smelling like a bottle of Jack Daniels. I had to use the radio. He couldn't see straight to tune the dial."

"Is someone coming?"

Jake locked the door behind him and they both sat on the bench. He had the bag he'd packed with them and took out a thermos.

"I contacted Forest Dispatch. They're sending everyone up. It'll be awhile, though." Jake poured them both cups of hot water and added tea bags. He handed her one. "Here, you need to drink this. I have chocolate, too. It's good for shock."

"Isn't that from Harry Potter?"

The corner of Jake's mouth quirked. "I think the chocolate frogs were for after someone had encountered dementors."

"Right. Not quite the same."

He unwrapped a gold-foiled chocolate bar and broke off a chunk, which she accepted gratefully. It was smooth and milky on her tongue, and the familiar flavor calmed her nerves. The warm cup of tea in her hands helped, too.

They sat in silence for a few moments, eating chocolate and drinking tea. It was a cozy scene, except for the dead body floating in the pool outside. Couldn't forget that.

"Isn't Amos on the job? Who is he, anyway?"

"He is." Jake frowned. "He's just a kid, early twenties? Local guy. Normally he drains the pool after closing, so he'd be off shift until morning when he turns the tap on to refill it. Since we were coming tonight, I guess he went on a bender instead."

"He won't get in trouble for letting us swim, will he?"

Jake shook his head. "This is an understood job perk. Royce explained that to me."

"Why did Royce tell you that? I thought he handled housing?"

"He's technically in the engineering department. He handles the upkeep of the government housing and compound, but he has his hands in everything across the Forest, it seems. He manages the winter grooming program, too."

"Isn't he a reserve sheriff's deputy? He'll probably be the first one up the mountain."

Jake shifted uneasily.

"What?"

He wouldn't meet her eyes.

"Jake?"

He took a sip of tea and looked into the distance.

"You're scaring me."

He exhaled heavily and put down his tea, finally meeting her gaze.

"I...think it might be Royce in the pool."

* * *

It took close to an hour and a half for the first responders to arrive. By then, Sadie and Jake had hiked back to the groomer and were sitting inside it, engine running and heater on full blast. Sadie had kept her eyes resolutely ahead as she'd walked by, refusing to peer in and see if she could recognize the short, squat body of Royce Hensley in the pool. Her mind whirled with what she'd seen in the parking lot this morning, wondering if it could be connected. It had to be, right? It was too big of a coincidence to see someone get into a fight in the morning and the same person dead later that night. Elaina had said Jerry was out on bail. He could've done this. They all lived at the bottom of the trail. And, Sadie remembered with a start, they'd seen Cole on the trail, too, pretty late. There were two suspects, both Jake's neighbors.

Even with all that on her mind, Sadie and Jake were quiet while they waited. When they finally saw lights coming around the bend, Jake got out to meet them. It was a trio of snowmobiles, and Sadie recognized the first figure that got off as Elaina. Of course, she lived at Poplar too. She guessed the other two were sheriff's deputies. Elaina acknowledged her grimly in the groomer as she walked by, Jake leading them to the pool. One deputy stayed back, and Sadie appreciated that. Amos was nowhere to be seen, probably sucking down coffee and trying to get sober. Or he was passed out. Either seemed an option, considering the state Jake had found him in.

It didn't take long for Jake to come back to the groomer. He climbed in with her and settled in wearily. "I asked if we could head back to my house and if they could question us there, but Elaina said we had to stick around."

Sadie had guessed that would be the case.

"This was probably an accident, right?" She asked Jake finally.

Jake stared off into the distance again.

"Are you okay, Jake?"

He shook himself. "I don't know. It's...if it is Royce, there's a lot of people that hated him. But I didn't see anything that made me think it wasn't an accident. Some...blood, but that could've been from falling, right?"

"Yes."

"It was probably an accident. You're right."

Sadie thought about the locked gate. Why lock the gate after yourself? Why be there at all? If it was an accident, when had it happened, and why hadn't Amos seen anything? Sadie reached a gloved hand out and put it over his. The seats in the groomer were far apart with a wide console between them, and she couldn't reach him to hug him. She wished she could.

It was another hour before Elaina came back to take their statements. By then, a snowcat had arrived and a group of people in heavy duty snow clothes had gotten out and spread across the scene. The snowcat had brought a sledded trailer full of equipment. Soon lights were being erected, and barriers were placed at the entrance to the parking lot. The quiet, snow-covered, magical moonlit scene of their arrival was gone. The moon had gone behind thick clouds, and the bustle signaled something very wrong had happened at Pritchard Hot Springs.

* * *

Elaina broke the news that they couldn't take the groomer home.

"You might erase evidence. We came up your untouched groomer track. The other side is as it was."

"So this wasn't an accident, then?" Sadie asked.

Elaina eyed her, then shrugged. "It wasn't. Someone did this."

They were both silent while they considered that.

"It wasn't us," Sadie finally said, to fill the silence.

"The evidence so far indicates that, but we'll need to corroborate it with your statements and witness statements that show the timing you came up here."

"There's a GPS tracker on the groomer," Jake said. "That will give you exact timing. Royce–"

"Is dead." Elaina interrupted without inflection. Sadie gasped. Jake buried his head in his hands. "We'll get the tracking information from someone else. I'm sorry to be the one to tell you, and for you to find out like this, and to keep you here." Elaina sounded truly regretful, the first emotion she'd let into her voice all night.

"We're exhausted, Elaina," Jake said finally, lifting his head from his hands.

"I know. You'll go back in the snowcat as soon as I take your statements."

Statement-giving was tedious work, as Sadie remembered from this afternoon when she'd given her statement on the parking lot fight to Elaina. She felt a twinge of apprehension giving a statement without her lawyer, Paige's husband, Mateo, present, but she hoped he'd forgive her when she confessed later. After all, she really had nothing to hide.

Jake and Sadie tried to be patient as they answered the same questions again and again with no new information being uncovered. No, they hadn't seen anything suspicious until they were about to get in the water. Yes, they'd noticed the abandoned snowmobile. No, they hadn't heard or seen anything else.

When Elaina asked if they'd seen anyone coming down the trail as they went up, Sadie and Jake glanced at each other, and then Jake admitted that they'd seen Cole on the way down. Elaina hadn't reacted to this news, stoically writing it down. After what felt like an hour, they were finally free to go. They gathered their things, then climbed into the snowcat, a boxy orange thing on tracks with bench seats in the back that could be folded to hold gear. The deputy that drove it was friendly, making sure the heater was blowing full blast at them, and they proceeded down the trail in silence.

It was two o'clock in the morning when they made it back to Jake's truck. Sadie wouldn't drive back to Jackson this late. She had to be at the coffee kiosk by six o'clock. As they drove into the circle of houses that made up Poplar, Sadie noticed lights on in most windows. Word was out something had happened to one of their own. What remained to be seen was if one of their neighbors was the murderer.

# Chapter Five

Sadie arrived at the coffee kiosk ten minutes late. Kendall was grooving to her favorite folktronica playlist. She took one look at Sadie and pointed at the door.

"Nope. I'm not having a zombie moose in here today. It's a Saturday, babe. It's not going to be busy. Go back to Jake's warm bed and sleep it off."

"It's not what you think," Sadie protested, putting on an apron and washing her hands.

"Oh no, it's exactly what I think." Kendall's hands worked the espresso machine deftly.

"No, Kendall, it's murder. Hot springs murder."

"Of Royce Hensley." She handed a shocked Sadie a drink carrier with two coffees and a pile of baked goods stuffed in the other compartments. "Take this. Crawl back into bed with that hunky man. Drink the coffees and eat the food when you wake up in a few more hours. Then come back here and tell me everything."

"It's more likely you'll tell me what I haven't already found out."

"Probably." A car horn beeped outside and Kendall's nostrils flared.

"I don't know what I'd do without you, Kendall," Sadie said, deciding not to fight her. Where Kendall got her information was a mystery. Her control and competence in every aspect of her life made her a force of nature. Plus, she was hot, a star and influencer on LGBTQIA+ TikTok, and dating a billionaire almost-mob-princess. Sadie knew it was only a matter of time before she lost Kendall to something bigger and better than being her barista, but she was going to treasure every minute she had her. "But be nice to the customers, even the annoying honky ones."

"Oh, I'll be nice," Kendall threatened, turning to the window with a fake smile on her face. "I'll be nice as I upsell him the entire bakery case for his impertinence."

Sadie walked out the back door to the sound of Kendall making a joke and the man in the car laughing. He was going to buy everyone at his destination pastries, and he didn't even know it yet.

It was dark in the room, like early evening, when Sadie woke up for the second time that Saturday. Panicking, she scrabbled for her phone on the bedside table, turning the screen on to see it was only ten o'clock. Jake made a noise beside her and she turned to look at him. He was shirtless, his eyes still resolutely closed, arm thrown over his face in protest. Last night, when they'd finally crawled into bed, they'd both fallen asleep immediately. When Sadie had come back to his bed this morning, he'd welcomed her into his warm embrace, and Sadie had drifted off surrounded by his heat. It was tempting, considering the dark of the room probably meant it was snowing outside, to crawl back in with him, but she needed to get to the coffee kiosk to help Kendall close up for the weekend. They were closed on Sundays, and then she needed to go to the bakery. Plus, she wanted a shower. Sighing, Sadie leaned over to Jake and planted a kiss on his cheek.

"I'll call you later," she whispered, and he grumbled something intelligible. She'd forgotten what a grouchy sleeper he was. She crept out of the darkened bedroom, used the bathroom, and pulled on the change of clothes she'd brought with her. Tyrone looked up from his bed by the crackling wood stove and she gave him head scratches. She'd fed him this morning before she'd left the first time. She took a few minutes to reheat the coffee Kendall had made for her earlier, then poured it back into the paper cup, took her share of pastries, and stepped out onto Jake's front porch. Tyrone slipped past her to stretch on the deck. She locked the door behind her. Because she was working at the coffee kiosk, Jake had given her a key in case she needed a place nearby. Poplar was only a five-minute drive from the Junction.

Outside, everything was white. Low, dark clouds were dumping big, fluffy snowflakes rapidly, the kind of snow that accumulated into feet overnight. She hoped the plows were out so she could travel into town without trouble. As she stood under the covered porch, watching the snow accumulate and Tyrone frolic about in it, she sipped her coffee. She needed to clean off her Subaru, already covered in several inches since this morning, but she needed more caffeine first.

She peered around the neighborhood. With the snow so thick, she couldn't see every residence in the circle. From what she could see, since it was a weekend day, most residences had vehicles in their driveways. Lights were on inside, and smoke billowed from the wood stove chimneys. All the houses used wood stoves for heat, requiring hours of time in summer and fall collecting and processing wood to get them through the winter. Since Jake had moved in after processing was complete and snow was on the ground, he'd had to buy a load from Royce. He hadn't been happy at the price he'd paid, declaring it a rip off.

Thinking of Royce, Sadie's heart sank. She couldn't believe they'd found him dead last night. She looked around the neighborhood again. It was probable, maybe even likely, that the person who had killed Royce was in one of these houses. Maybe even right this minute. It was a frightening thought, and it spurred Sadie off the porch and down to her car, whistling for Tyrone.

* * *

Kendall reported that the morning had been slow, then got slower when the snow started. Seeing how few cars were on the road, Sadie decided to close early, and they worked together to close the shop, bumping to a nineties R&B playlist while they did. In between verses of TLC's Waterfalls, Kendall told Sadie everything she'd heard about the murder.

"Elaina came by looking exhausted, but she was tight lipped."

"As expected. I think since the murder happened on Forest Service land, she's probably leading the investigation."

"She said as much. At least for now."

"What do you mean by that?"

"Well, Penny came by on the way to Idaho Falls for a vintage clothing expo." Penny Dwyer was Sadie's childhood friend and the office manager and occasional reporter for the Jackson Hole Journal.

"I'm surprised she was out in this weather." For being born and raised in a place that regularly got over 400 inches of snow a year, Penny stayed as far away from it as she could.

Kendall snorted. "She had Officer Greg Knott himself driving her in his Jeep."

Sadie laughed. "Of course she did."

"I think she actually likes him," Kendall protested.

"She likes him giving her information, driving her around, and taking her out to fancy dinners, that's for sure." Sadie felt a pang and realized she was being unkind to one of her oldest friends. "Maybe she does like him. He's not who I think of as her type–"

"What would Penny's type be? A vampire?"

"She's usually gone for vintage-dressing rock stars. Come to think of it, at least one of them, her name was Drisella, could've been a vampire as well as an electric violinist."

"I agree with you, though. I think she might like the straight-laced Officer Knott."

They were quiet for a minute while they both pictured the rockabilly styled, flamboyantly dressed, dramatic always, rotating rainbow-haired Penny with a man whose personality seemed to comprise being a cop, hunting, and drinking Bud Light.

"Someone for everyone, I guess," Kendall said finally while she loaded the leftover pastries into a box to transport to town. She'd take them to the self-serve food pantry box recently installed at the Episcopal church near town square.

"I guess. Perhaps he has depths we don't know about. Anyway, what did she have to say?" Sadie lifted the mop out of the bucket and started mopping backwards towards the door, Kendall behind her.

"Right. She said since Royce worked for the Forest Service and was also a reserve deputy, both agencies might give the investigation over to a neutral third party."

"Oh, shit," Sadie said, recognizing what that meant.

Kendall grinned at her, her white teeth forming a fierce

edifice. "You're going to have to work with Detective Will Nolan again, ooh la la."

Detective Nolan had been the investigator in charge of the case Sadie had found herself in the middle of last fall. He hadn't been too keen on her doing her own investigation. He'd also thought she was the main suspect, failed to protect her from the actual killer, and had a hard time looking Sadie in the eye after she'd almost died—again—after exposing the murderer.

But in the six months since he'd joined the force, Sadie had noticed some positive changes in the local police department. Officers were coming into her bakery again, for one, after they'd stopped coming in once she put a Black Lives Matter sticker on the door. The department also had a new chief, and she'd taken important steps to ban brutal and unequal practices common in departments across the country. Sadie was hopeful the change would be permanent, and had recently advocated at a city council meeting for re-appropriating funding from the department into social safety nets.

She'd expected a bigger fall out, but the next day Officer Knott had come to the bakery to get two dozen muffins for a staff meeting. Either the department truly was changing, or Penny was a good influence. Kendall thought the detective had a crush on her, which was ridiculous. More likely, he felt guilty arresting the wrong person had led to her almost dying.

"He won't like that I'm involved in this." That was putting it mildly. Kendall turned off the music and opened the back door. She inched out onto the top step to make room. Sadie opened the door to their tiny pantry and emptied the mop bucket into the drain on the floor, then rinsed the mop out.

She turned out the lights and stepped outside, locking the door and setting the alarm using her key chain fob. One thing that had come from her first brush with murder, she was much more security conscious in her everyday life. She even remembered to charge her doorbell alarm battery. Most of the time.

It was still snowing, and Kendall and Sadie had to work to brush the snow off their cars. Kendall's had almost a foot on it. Sadie glanced at the reader board across the highway that showed road closures, and saw everything was open, at least for now. She waved bye to Kendall and climbed inside her car, snowflakes in her eyelashes and dotting her purple ski jacket. Tyrone sat up from the backseat where she'd covered him up with a blanket before going inside, woofing low in greeting. Then she started her car and pulled out after Kendall, fingers gripped tightly on the wheel.

# Chapter Six

Sadie slunk in the back door of the bakery thirty minutes before closing. She'd almost decided not to come after the harrowing drive into town. While her and Kendall had kept all four tires on the road, that hadn't been the case for other drivers. First responders had been at each accident, so Sadie and Kendall had crept by without stopping, but she'd been nervous until she parked in her garage and settled Tyrone. The bakery was only two blocks from her house, so she walked over after clearing her own sidewalks, stomping through the heavy snow, the sounds of town muffled under the thick blanket of white.

Only Max Ridgely, her first assistant baker, was in the kitchen. Sadie could hear her weekend barista, Rachael Simms, chatting away with a customer through the passthrough. It sounded quiet out there. Everyone was probably either home or up at one of the three nearby ski resorts skiing freshies. Sadie wondered if she could get a few turns in at Snow King, the town hill that loomed above Jackson, before dark, but dismissed it. She had work to catch up on.

"Another murder, boss? Really?" Max asked as she took off

her coat and hung it up. Max was non-binary and used they/them pronouns. They were Northern Arapahoe and had grown up on the Wind River Reservation in Central Wyoming. When Sadie had found herself in a tight spot after her previous assistant baker was forced out of the valley by her landlord doubling her rent, Kendall had brought new-to-town Max to the bakery, and they'd basically never left. After a few weeks, Sadie had promoted them to Assistant Baker, and it was the best decision she'd ever made.

"The worst of luck," Sadie said, stomping off her boots and changing into her kitchen shoes before heading to the hand washing sink.

"You're like Jessica Fletcher."

"I always thought she was the most likely suspect after all those murders."

"It was obvious. She had serious old lady killer vibes."

They laughed together, and Sadie came to see what they were working on. Max loomed over her as she peered into the mixer. They were over six feet tall, whip-thin with baker's arms and shoulders, and had black hair that was long on the top and shaved on the sides. With their burnished skin and sharp features, they cut an imposing figure, but it hid the teddy bear they were inside.

"Yet another batch of sugar cookie dough," Max said. "There's a few more things to prep, but it was slow enough today we won't have to stay very late."

"Speak for yourself," Sadie sighed as she eyed the mostly crossed-off list attached by a magnet to the fridge. "I have to do the books."

"Not before you talk to your table of regulars," Rachael interrupted, sticking her head through the passthrough. Her signature high blonde ponytail swung in agitation. She opened her eyes wide to emphasize. "They will not leave and they're driving me bananas."

Sadie grimaced. Right. She should've known she'd have to face her table of regulars once the news got out. They were seven women, all pillars of the community that were old enough to have leisure time. They usually arrived at opening at seven o'clock and stayed through the morning rush while taking up the biggest and best table in the corner that overlooked the board-walk. The women whispered and cackled and drank coffee and passed their judgements on the town and solved the world's problems at that table. Sadie put up with them because they meant well, held an unknown but not imaginary amount of power, and were some of her best custom order customers. For them to have stayed until almost closing at two o'clock meant things were dire. Millie Yin, the oldest of the group, who had been old when Sadie was a kid, napped most afternoons.

"Sorry Rach." Sadie stepped through the swinging door and entered the main dining room. Moose's was a small historical cabin that had been built onto in the seventies to make it into a restaurant. Her parents, Arlo and Robin, had bought it when the restaurant closed and converted it into a bakery. The front room was the original cabin, with eight tables and seating for around twenty-five. Where other local businesses had updated from the log cabin look to whitewashed walls and modern fixtures, Moose's leaned into it. The stripped knotty pine shone, and there were knotty pine tables and chairs. The bakery case gleamed. While Sadie had installed the espresso machine and upgraded to a modern point of sale system, she hadn't made too many other changes. There were vegan and gluten-free treats on the menu now, and they served a light soup and sandwich lunch. And, most importantly to Sadie, her employees earned a living wage with a housing allowance and health and leave benefits. But the sugar cookies were the same ones her Grandma

Moose, and then her dad, had made, even if sometimes they made them in shapes coinciding with TikTok trends.

Today, only two tables were occupied. One two-top with a pair of wide-eyed tourists who kept exclaiming out the window about the snow in German, and the other by her white-haired table of regulars. And they were all looking at her, all seven wrinkly faces, glasses perched on their noses. Squaring her shoulders, Sadie smiled and walked over to them. They pulled out a seat for her next to Opal Fowler, their short, designer-track-suit-wearing leader.

"Sadie," Opal began, brushing an invisible piece of lint off her purple velour tracksuit. A snuffle under the table caused her to stop and Sadie gave her a look.

"I've told you more than once you can't bring Prada in here. No dogs allowed, even if they fit in your bag and sleep most of the day."

"We had to wait so long for you!" Opal exclaimed. Sadie was opening her mouth to protest once again, because the health inspector would not be happy, but a sob interrupted them. Sadie swiveled her eyes to the source of the noise.

"You have to help me," Lilith Dormer sobbed, her hands over her mouth making her muffled. With her head downcast, her sharp widow's peak stood out. She was missing her signature many clacking bracelets, which Sadie wasn't sure she'd ever seen her without.

"There, there," Denise Garza said, putting down her knit-ting to drape an arm around Lilith's shaking shoulders. "Sadie's here and she'll help you."

Sadie gulped. "I...what's wrong, Lilith?"

"It's–" another sob cut her off.

"It's her grandson, Amos Garner," Zoey Fremont filled in. She worked as a summer interpretive ranger at Grand Teton National Park, just up the road from Jackson. She was plainspoken and known for her sharp tongue, but could always be trusted to speak the truth.

"Amos is your grandson?" Sadie asked, surprised. She'd never even heard the name Amos until yesterday morning, and now he was everywhere.

"Yes," Lilith said, lifting her head and mopping her eyes with a handkerchief Gretchen Whitehouse pulled out of her I ♥ Bodice Rippers tote bag. "My daughter Jeanie's youngest. He's such a sweet boy–" her voice hitched, "but that awful Detective Nolan thinks he killed Royce Hensley!" She dissolved into sobs again.

Sadie mulled that over while Denise and Chloe Fremont, Zoey's younger, more kind-worded sister, comforted Lilith. So Detective Nolan was in charge of the investigation because of the conflicts of interest, just like Penny had thought. And Amos was the number one suspect! Sadie thought about what she remembered from last night and decided it was plausible. Amos had cleaned the changing rooms, locked up behind him, but not seen the dead body in the pool? Then, knowing that Jake and her were headed up, he got wasted to avoid questioning? Sadie wondered at the manner of Royce's death. Was there a weapon involved? Had he been drowned? Jake had said he'd seen blood, though.

Sadie shook herself. She didn't need to wonder these things, because she was absolutely not getting involved in another murder investigation. The last one had almost killed her—twice! Three times if she counted being almost run over to scare off the killer pointing a gun at her. Sadie was a respectable business-woman, an activist for housing and social justice, a dog mom, a baker. She didn't need to be running around like a mystery hero-ine, finding dead bodies and then solving the crimes. Plus, who had the time, really?

"You just have to help me," Lilith was saying again, her voice wobbly as her eyes implored Sadie. "He's a good kid."

"I'm sure he is," Sadie said gently. "Last night after we found the body, Jake went to get him and he was absolutely wasted, though. Maybe something happened he doesn't remember?"

Lilith sat up a little straighter. "My Amos has had some trouble in the past with alcohol, but he's been clean for close to a year. One reason he took that job this winter was to stay away from the temptations his no good ski bum friends succumb too every night at the bars."

"I respect that. Anyone can slip in their recovery, and though I didn't see Amos, Jake told me he smelled like a bottle of Jack Daniels."

"Amos says he remembers nothing after cleaning the changing rooms. He swears he didn't take a drop of liquor! They tested his blood. I bet you anything it comes back clean."

That was interesting. If Amos hadn't drank, why was he nonsensical? What, exactly, did he remember about cleaning the changing rooms? Was he saying he didn't see Royce that night? Sadie's fingers itched for a sharpened #2 Dixon Ticonderoga pencil and a fresh pad of paper so she could write out her questions, draw a diagram or two. This was a puzzle that could be solved if someone asked the right questions. And Sadie knew that if Amos had been in trouble before, he could become a suspect just for that. With a start, she realized she was falling into investigative mode.

She stood. "I'm really sorry, Lilith. But I can't. It's not my place."

Opal stood as well. "But we voted on it."

"You...voted on if I would help Lilith?" Opal had told her once that she kept the number at the table to seven so no votes could end in a tie, but had gotten tight lipped when asked what, exactly, they had to vote on.

"Yes. We voted we would ask this of you. We don't ask a lot, Sadie." Opal's tone reminded her of Grandma Moose's when she would admonish Sadie for not calling more while she was away at college. Sadie examined each face. Opal looked stern. Lilith broken, tears still streaming from her eyes. Denise had picked up her knitting, but was looking right at her as the needles clacked. Gretchen, Chloe, and Zoey looked friendly, but firm. Millie Yin was asleep. And they were right. They asked little of her. They supported her business, defended her to her detractors, kept her informed of what the competition was doing. All they asked was that she come out to visit and occasionally do a favor. And this time the favor was clearing the name of a wayward grandson.

Sadie sighed. "Fine. I'll meet with Amos and see if there's anything to follow up on."

Lilith collapsed in relief, and Opal nodded at her.

"But if there's not anything to follow up on, I'm done," Sadie warned. They didn't meet her eyes, but they nodded their assent, gathering their things and moving to leave. The bakery was closed. They'd stayed all day and gotten what they wanted. Sadie hoped she wasn't in for more than she'd promised.

# Chapter Seven

Sunday dawned clear and bright, the sun reflecting off the new fallen snow and blinding anyone daring enough to look directly at it. Sadie slept until Tyrone jumped on top of her, begging to be let out. He'd once had a doggy door that opened or closed if his collar was nearby. That had proved to be a bigger security weakness than the old doggy door that had let squirrels nest in her chimney, so she'd had to block it off permanently. Now Sadie made sure she, KitKat, or one of the O'Donnells, the nice family she was leasing the house on the other side of the alley to, could let Tyrone out when needed. Luckily, he was a charming moose, and everyone liked to help.

Sadie released Tyrone into the backyard to romp in the snow, then started her coffeemaker and filled Tyrone's food and water bowls. Nothing was on the schedule for the day. The coffee kiosk was closed, and Max had opened at the bakery. Sage Wallace, her new second assistant baker, would relieve them mid-morning, and Rachael would cover the front all day. Sundays in the winter were normally quiet after the initial rush to get breakfast before hitting the slopes, and on a day like today, with feet of fresh snow overnight, everyone would rush to the resorts to try to snag first chair.

She opened her front door and grabbed the Jackson Hole Journal off her porch. Her sidewalk and paths were already cleared, and she bet she had KitKat to thank for that. She let Tyrone in, giving him a head scratch before he trotted over to his food bowl to inhale his breakfast. She sat down at her kitchen counter with a cup of coffee and the paper.

To Sadie's surprise, the front page above the fold main story wasn't Royce's murder, but a story on a recent wildlife trapping and tagging project the Forest Service and National Park Service had collaborated on in Grand Teton National Park. The main photo was of an enormous wolf lying on a tarp with a green-clad man checking their teeth. The wolf's eyes were slit open, looking at the man. Sadie read the caption.

"Bridger-Teton National Forest Wildlife Biologist Carl Brent collars a large male wolf, part of the Phantom Springs pack, after it had been tranquilized and transported to the project site last Wednesday."

Sadie shivered. Better him than her. She knew the wolf had been lovingly cared for before being transported back to their habitat, albeit with a collar around their neck so wildlife biologists could study its movements. Still, she was glad she wasn't in the business of being so close to barely tranquilized wild animals. Sadie's close encounter with a grizzly bear last fall still haunted her nightmares.

Sadie flipped through the paper and found a short notice about a body being found in Pritchard Hot Springs on page three. The article didn't tell her anything she didn't already know. Small town news. Sadie finished her coffee and her stomach growled.

What Sadie wanted was breakfast. And not what she could make from the meager items in her fridge. She found her phone and scrolled through her contacts. She scrolled past Jake. He'd texted last night saying he'd gotten his groomer back and would be out all night on the other trails, so not to expect to hear from him until late afternoon. And she scrolled past Penny, who had stayed overnight in Idaho Falls last night with Officer Knott according to a story she'd seen on Instagram. Honestly, they'd looked cute in the slightly blurry late-night selfie, and Sadie was warming to the idea of the two of them together. She scrolled back up to Paige Gates-Ortiz and sent a text.

`Brunch at the Ten Gallon Hat?`

She didn't wait long, an ecstatic "YASSSS see you in 30" coming through almost immediately. Paige was in the second trimester of her first pregnancy and wanted to eat everything. A second text popped up.

`You have to let me smell your mimosa`

Sadie laughed and put her phone down. She put her coffee cup in the sink, then went to take a shower to get ready for her bestie brunch, Tyrone following behind her.

* * *

After a quick perusal of the menu, Paige ordered almost one of everything. Sadie ordered what she didn't order and was prepared to share. It was busy at the Ten Gallon Hat, the local's longtime favorite for breakfast just off the town square in downtown Jackson. They'd been lucky to grab a table for two near the back, where they didn't get as cold every time the front door opened. The long wooden counter was packed shoulder to shoulder with patrons. Sadie counted five pricey Canada Goose parkas, one cowboy hat, one wool bomber hat—overkill, really, it wasn't that cold—and one genuine fur coat perched on the stools. There was a scruffy man in the corner wearing a hat and sunglasses with a glamorous brunette, and Sadie narrowed her eyes at them. She was pretty sure the man had been in a big budget action film last summer. Celebrities loved Jackson Hole and could usually enjoy the town with little fanfare. Sadie averted her gaze. They were just trying to eat breakfast like the rest of them. She wouldn't stare, but she was definitely checking out the star's Instagram later. Conversation and cutlery clinking on plates filled the cozy restaurant, and they had to lean in close to talk to one another. Sadie smelled frying bacon and her stomach growled.

Paige wrapped her hands around a heavy white ceramic mug with the cafe's oversized cowboy hat logo on it and inhaled the coffee aroma, her brown eyes closing in bliss. Then she sighed and passed it over to Sadie.

"Still can't handle it?" Sadie took a sip. They used the same local roaster that Sadie did, and the familiar flavor was dark but pleasant.

"It's the only thing that still makes me want to puke. I even ate mushrooms the other day!"

Paige's first trimester had been rough, with little staying down. There'd been an entire month where she'd lived on rolls Sadie had baked for her every day. Now that she was in the second trimester, though, she was feeling better and was ready to make up for her previous limited diet. Sadie examined her friend. She was slim, but pregnancy had rounded not only her belly but also her oval face. Her normally pale complexion glowed, and her strawberry blonde hair had grown along with her belly. Pregnancy became her, and Sadie was excited to be an honorary auntie.

Someone walked up to their table and Sadie glanced up, not recognizing the cowboy-hatted man. They had eyes only for Paige.

"Councilwoman Gates-Ortiz," the man said, sticking out his hand. "I'm Preston Chandler."

Sadie saw Paige's face switch from friendly and relaxed to blank and professional. Her town-councilwoman-dealing-with-a-constituent face.

"Mr. Chandler," she said, shaking his hand firmly. "It's nice to meet you. Is there something I can help you with?"

"I don't want to disturb you ladies," Preston said, turning a wide Cheshire Cat smile Sadie's way and winking at her. Sadie blanched as soon as he looked away. Gross. She took in his outfit as he continued to talk to Paige. He was white, in his fifties, with salt and pepper hair and a handlebar mustache. He wore fancy cowboy boots that would have zero traction in the snow, pressed jeans, a western-style sherpa-lined coat, and an oversized white cowboy hat, much like the type the cafe was named for. Sadie could see the glint of an expensive watch on his wrist and a signet ring on his thumb. Everything about him screamed not from around here. Even in Jackson, cowboys wore snow boots when it snowed.

"I'd be happy to meet with you about that," Paige was saying, her smile forced. Preston handed her a business card.

"I'm so glad to hear it. I'll be in touch next week if I don't hear from you before then. You ladies have a great breakfast, now. The chicken fried steak is great." He tipped his absurdly enormous hat at them, then turned and walked away, out the door.

Sadie made a face as Paige sighed and put the card in her wallet.

"Who was that guy?"

"A developer, of course."

"Of fucking course."

"He has a piece of land down by Hoback Junction. He wants to talk about selling it to the county."

"You're on the town council, though."

Paige shrugged. "Yeah, but the deal he wants would involve

moving the fairgrounds from town to the property, and he'd get a cut of the housing we'd replace the fairgrounds with. He'd need both council's support."

Sadie whistled low. That had been proposed for years. The Teton County Fairgrounds took up a lot of valuable real estate in the town of Jackson, but also brought in a lot of revenue from the nightly rodeos from Memorial Day to Labor Day, fair, concerts, and sports activities. It was a decisive topic with lots of pros and cons. Even Sadie, who was active in the local housing action group and spoke out often about housing and workforce issues wasn't sure what the right answer was.

"That's pretty far out of town."

"No one is ever going to go for it." Paige rolled her eyes and sipped her herbal tea. "But I'll meet with him."

"Speaking of Hoback Junction…"

"Right! Tell me all about your latest murder, my little Miss Marple."

So Sadie did. The food arrived, and after Paige sniffed Sadie's mimosa, they dug into their dishes. Eggs Benedict with lemony hollandaise sauce, biscuits with spicy sausage gravy, a fluffy Belgian waffle piled with berries and whipped cream, an omelet with cream cheese, smoked salmon, and capers, home fries with bomba sauce and crispy fried hash browns. No chicken fried steak, though Paige had debated about it before deciding to order a side of bacon instead. They ate until they were stuffed while Sadie filled Paige in about seeing Royce fight with Jerry, finding Royce, Detective Nolan being in charge, and her table of regulars strong arming her into investigating to clear Amos's name. Paige mostly listened, exclaiming now and then between bites.

When they'd mostly cleared the plates, Paige leaned back, hands on her rounded belly, and laughed as the baby kicked. "Little one loves food as much as me," she said, taking one last sip of tea. "You know, I think a few months ago I would've been annoyed that your table of regulars was so pushy about this. But when I think about what I would do to help this baby, not knowing anything about them except that they live inside me and I love them, I get it. Lilith must be beside herself worrying about her grandson."

"She was," Sadie admitted. She examined the plates in front of her, deciding on what she wanted her last bite to be. "He's supposed to call me today so we can meet up. I have a lot of questions."

"From what I know about Royce, it sounds like a lot of people didn't care for him."

"Even Jake didn't like him," Sadie agreed, forking together one last bite of eggs Benedict and crispy hash brown. It was her favorite breakfast dish. She wondered how she could recreate the flavor in a pastry. An eggs benedict quiche in a hash brown crust? She was rolling around the idea of a hash brown burrito stuffed with egg and ham and hollandaise when Paige laughed.

"What?"

"I was talking to you, and you were completely blissed out, chewing. Thinking about a new recipe again?"

"You know it. What'd I miss?"

"I was asking if you've met Carl Brent, who lives down at Poplar."

Why did Sadie know that name? Oh right, the article. "I just saw him on the front page of the paper. I didn't know he lived at Poplar." She'd met a few residents, but not that many, mostly just waved at them now and then.

"He's a nice man. In his late forties. He lost his wife to cancer almost a year ago. You remember the benefit at the bowling alley?"

Sadie remembered. She'd donated mini cheesecakes and cookies for the buffet, and had spent too much on a spa day auction item she hadn't had time to use yet. It had been a great success, but Sadie remembered that the frail, petite woman in a bright head wrap they'd honored had died shortly after, the experimental treatment they'd raised money for having come too late.

"I didn't realize he lived down there. That was so sad."

"It was. He knew Royce, so I've been wondering how he's doing."

"I'll ask Jake to check in on him."

They paid the bill then, Paige insisting on paying since she ordered so much food, and boxed up their leftovers. As they did, Paige looked up at Sadie suddenly, earnestly.

"Promise me you won't get in trouble with all this," she said in a small voice. "I need you around long term to help me with this whole mom thing."

Sadie reached out and covered her friend's hand. "I promise you. I will be safe, and I won't poke my nose in too far. I learned my lesson last time."

# Chapter Eight

Sadie heard from Amos while she was doing laundry that afternoon. She finished loading the dryer, then studied the text he'd sent.

This is Amos Garner. My Gran told me to text you. I'm in town if you can meet up.

Sadie checked her watch. It was one o'clock. Not too late for coffee and the bakery was still open.

Hi Amos. Meet me at Moose's Bakery in 30?

She got a thumbs up back immediately, which she supposed passed for a yes.

Fifteen minutes later, she was walking in the back door of the bakery. It smelled like sugar cookies, and Sadie smiled to herself. It was the most familiar fragrance of her childhood, and it always made her happy. Even when she mixed hundreds of pounds of it a week. The kitchen was empty, so Sadie slipped into her office unnoticed. She needed to pull the information for tomorrow's barista interviews. She had enough time to print out the resumes and hiring paperwork she'd need.

As she did, she glanced over the resumes again. She was interviewing six people. Three of them listed Jackson addresses, and two of them listed addresses in Hoback Junction. One listed an address that was familiar to her—Pritchard Hot Springs Road. She looked at it closer. It was for Holly Richards, who must be the pretty blonde wife of Cole. Interesting.

"Moose, there's a shifty guy here to see you," Sage said from the doorway. Sadie jumped.

"Sorry," Sage apologized, the dangly beaded earrings she wore clicking together as she shook her head at her.

"Thanks, Sage." Sadie gathered everything into a folder and shoved it into her bag and smiled grimly at the tawny skinned, lithe, curly haired woman. "I was expecting him."

Amos Garner did look shifty. He sat at the corner table for two, overlooking the boardwalk, his back to the wall. He was probably about Sadie's height, white, and slender. His black hair was in his eyes, and he kept sweeping it out of the way. He was dressed all in black, but for the weather, at least. His gaze darted around the bakery. His leg bounced up and down rapidly under the table. He had white earbuds in his ears and Sadie wondered what he was listening to. Either way, he looked like he was about to bolt.

Sadie approached the table before he could.

"Amos?"

"Yes. Ms. Moose?" His voice was polite, and Sadie smiled warmly at him before sitting down.

"Yes. Can I get you something to drink or eat?"

"No, that's okay."

"Are you sure? I'm going to have a coffee. Rachael's bringing me one."

"A tea? I don't need any more caffeine. My heart's racing," he confessed, finally meeting her eyes. When he did, Sadie saw that despite the shifty goth kid persona, he was looking at her earnestly, and his eyes were full of panic.

"I'll order you one," she said, getting up. "I'll be right back."

When she returned, he looked just as nervous.

"You know I was with Jake that night?" Sadie dived right in.

Amos nodded miserably. "Yes. I knew he was bringing someone with him, but I didn't know who. I found out later it was you."

"It was nice of you to keep the hot springs open for us," Sadie said kindly.

"It's part of the job. But Jake is chill. I was happy to do it for him."

"Tell me about the job."

Rachael brought their drinks and a platter of sugar cookies and put them down, her blonde ponytail swinging as always. Sadie gestured at him to help himself, and he took a snowflake shaped cookie with blue frosting and nibbled it before replying.

"It was pretty easy. I made sure people paid and cleaned the bathrooms and changing rooms. With all the snow, it got pretty messy with people tracking it in, but it wasn't too bad. Then at night, I would drain the pool and spray it down. In the morning, I'd set it to fill again. I worked on and off in short blocks of time."

"Why'd you take the job?"

Amos's gaze flicked away, towards the towering ski slope of Snow King just visible over the buildings across the street.

"College wasn't for me. I came home and started working as a liftie, but I started partying a little hard."

Sadie took a sip of coffee. Lilith had alluded to as much. Being a liftie, or a lift operator, at a ski resort was one of the less prestigious roles at a ski hill. It was an entry level position that came with a ski pass and access to out-of-towners who liked to party.

"I started partying more than working, got fired, kept party-ing, and ended up getting in some trouble. When I got back to town, I wanted to do something different and not fall into the same bad habits. My Gran helped me get that job. It's through a concessionaire, not the Forest Service, and Gran knew someone who knew someone."

"I don't need more details," Sadie prefaced. "But what got you sent out of town for a bit, was it anything violent?"

"No! Absolutely not."

"Okay." Sadie paused. "Tell me about Friday, starting in the morning."

Amos finished his cookie and took a sip of tea, then took a deep breath. "It was a normal day. I filled the pool starting at six. People started showing up around ten when we open. I checked for payment stubs and patrolled on my usual schedule. It was busy. Quite a few big groups had come up with outfitters. At one point, I counted forty-seven people in the pool. It slowed down around four, and by five-thirty everyone was out of the pool and getting ready to head back down. I cleaned the changing rooms and bathrooms and the pool deck. I locked the combo gate behind me. And that's the last thing I remember until Jake knocked on my door."

He must have seen a look on her face.

"I swear it! I know you think I got wasted, but I swear I didn't! I didn't keep any alcohol up at the cabin, and I just got my green chip at AA for eleven months."

"I believe you," Sadie said, surprised to find that she did. "But that means something happened to you. Think back. Did you eat or drink something?"

Amos shut his eyes. "I've been trying to think, but it's all so fuzzy. I remember walking across the parking lot. I remember opening the door to my cabin. And that's it."

"Did you see a snowmobile parked in the lot when you went through it?"

"No."

Sadie sat up straighter. "You didn't? There was a snowmobile parked in the first row of parking when Jake and I got there."

"It wasn't there when I walked through the lot. I would've noticed, and I would've made a note about the make, model, color, and tag so I could report it to Elaina if it was still there the next night."

"When you woke up, what did you see?"

"I smelled, first. I woke up and my head was pounding, and I reeked of whiskey. I immediately ran to throw up in the bathroom. Then I answered the door, and it was Jake. I could tell he thought I'd been drinking, and I wanted to explain, but I was freaking out because of what he told me and because I couldn't remember anything."

"How much time had gone by?"

Amos considered. "I finished cleaning after eight. I took my time coming back because it was a beautiful night, so I probably went into my cabin around eight-thirty."

Sadie calculated. "So close to two hours. It was just after ten when we were getting into the hot springs. Was anything different in your cabin?"

"Yes. There was a half empty bottle of Jack Daniels and an empty mug on my table, and the fire had been built up because it was still going. And someone had doused me in Jack, because I reeked. And my erm–" He broke off, blushing.

"What?"

"My butt hurt. I have a big bruise on it. Maybe I slipped and fell?"

Sadie considered that.

"Do you think you drank any whiskey, even just by someone pouring it down your throat?"

Amos flicked his hair out of his eyes. "I didn't throw any up."

"Did they take your blood alcohol level?"

"I didn't blow anything on the Breathalyzer, but I consented to a blood test because they didn't believe that I hadn't been drinking. I haven't heard the results of that."

"Do you have a lawyer?"

"Gran got me one."

"Good."

Sadie went over the information she'd learned in her head. "When was the last time you saw Royce?"

Amos winced. "He'd been up Thursday afternoon in his official capacity to run the plow in the parking lot and fix a bench in the men's changing room."

"You didn't see him Friday?"

"No."

"Did you talk to him on Thursday?"

Amos rolled his eyes. "I hate to speak ill of the dead, but no one really talked to Royce. He talked at you, and you were lucky to get a word in edge wise."

Sadie was silent.

"But yes, I talked with him. He was checking to see how things were going."

"Did everything seem okay with him?"

"He seemed like his normal self. He was hassling me about wearing my AirPods while I worked. But like, it's boring work and I should be able to listen to podcasts if I want to. And he wasn't my boss."

"Did you ever fight with him?"

"Absolutely not. I knew better. He may not have been my boss, but he could cause trouble for me if he wanted. I mostly tried to stay out of his way."

Sadie couldn't think of anything else to ask. What could have happened to Amos for him to forget everything after he walked in to his cabin? Why would someone do that to him, anyway? So he wasn't a witness to the murder? To frame him for the murder? None of it made sense. They finished their drinks and talked a little about the weather, and then Amos stood to go.

"I appreciate you talking to me. Do you think you can help?"

"I'm not sure, but I'll think about it. I might ask some more questions. Text me if you find out anything else."

He agreed, then turned to go.

"Oh!" Sadie exclaimed, remembering. "Did you see Cole Richards at the hot springs on Friday?"

Amos's face closed. "I don't know who that is," he said after a pause, shrugging. He walked out the door. It was the first statement he'd made that day that sounded insincere to Sadie, and it made her stomach hurt.

* * *

"I think I messed up."

Sadie opened her front door wider, letting Penny, who'd uttered those words, through. "What do you mean, babe?" Sadie asked, shutting the front door and turning to her friend. Penny was dressed casually in black joggers stuffed into snow boots and a sweatshirt. Her pale face was clean of makeup, her normally rosy cheeks sallow. If Penny hadn't taken the time to do her normal cat eye makeup, it must be dire.

Penny was taking off her coat and boots, but when she looked back up at her, Sadie could see tears in her eyes. She pulled her into her arms. "What is it?"

Penny let herself be held for a minute before pulling away. "I'll tell you over wine. You have wine, right?"

"Of course I have wine. Go sit by the fire, I'll be there in a minute."

Sadie grabbed a bottle of red and two stemless glasses from the kitchen, meeting Penny in the living room where she'd settled onto one of the ancient leather couches. Sadie had purchased the house she'd grown up in from her parents when they'd moved to Arizona to retire. She hadn't changed much, from the red apple themed kitchen to the pink tile in the guest bathroom, but it was comfortable and felt like home.

Sadie chose the couch across from Penny and sat on the edge, uncorking the wine with the opener she'd brought with her. Penny had wiped her eyes and had a tissue clutched in her hand. Sadie poured them both glasses and handed one to her.

"Now tell me what happened."

Penny took a gulp of wine, then sighed, brushing her bright pink hair out of her eyes. "I caught feelings for Greg."

Sadie choked on her wine and put her glass down, sputtering. "Really?" She croaked.

Penny frowned. "Is it that surprising?"

Sadie coughed and struggled to get ahold of herself. "He doesn't seem like your type, but he seems nice?"

Penny's eyes filled with tears again. "He is nice. He's *nice to me.* And he asks me *how I'm doing.* And *how he can help me.* He shovels my walkway without asking. He asked me if he could take my car to get the oil changed. He's the most confusing man."

"Because he's nice to you?"

"Yes!"

Sadie sipped her wine and let her friend think that over for a minute.

"I guess I've just never been with someone who was...kind. And I didn't mean to get feelings for him, it just happened. But we're not well matched, at all."

"Opposites attract, right?"

Penny snorted. "He wears Skechers unironically. White ones. He drives a pickup truck named Delores. He watches

NASCAR and has a favorite baseball, football, and hockey team."

"No basketball?"

"Only college. I hate that I know that. He listens to country music about trucks and dogs and guns."

"All things that can be overlooked, if he's a good partner to you, though?"

Penny smiled wanly. "I hate to admit it, but he's great in bed."

"Well, that helps."

"But he's a cop."

Sadie shrugged. "You know what they say about bad apples. I don't think he is one. Do you think he's the kind of man that would stand up if he saw something bad happening, even among his colleagues?"

Penny took a sip of wine and stared into the fire. "I think so, but I don't know so. Not yet."

They sat in companionable silence for a while, sipping their wine and staring into the fire. Sadie couldn't help but let her thoughts drift to her own love life. She'd been having fun with Jake the past month, but was it really going anywhere? Life with a wildland firefighter for a boyfriend was tough. They were home all winter, but then once spring rolled around, they were gone until fall, popping in occasionally and unexpectedly until it snowed. And making the Forest Service a career usually meant moving around a lot to climb the career ladder. Would Jake stick around Jackson, or would he need to take a job somewhere else in a few years? Sadie wasn't leaving Jackson. This was her home, where her business was, where the friends that had become family were. And Jackson was a tough place for people to stay.

"Speaking of Officer Knott..." Sadie said finally, breaking the silence.

Penny blinked at her. "Oh, right. The case. You know they're looking at Amos Garner as a suspect?"

"I talked to him this afternoon. He's one of my regular's grandsons."

"Well, they had to rerun his blood labs because of some irregularities, which I thought was interesting."

"Hmmm. Amos insists he wasn't drinking. What else would make him pass out like that and not have any memory?"

"Roofies?"

"He said he didn't eat or drink anything."

"Chloroform?"

"Someone would have to hold a soaked cloth on his face for a long time to get it to work, I think. At least that's what I've read. It's not as simple as Ace Ventura made it look."

They both sat silent, stumped for a moment.

"But why go through all that trouble, anyway?" Sadie mused.

"So he wasn't a witness?"

"I suppose. Amos would've noticed if a snowmobile came up. But anyone would've. They're loud! But why kill Royce there? And why was Royce there in the first place?"

"Detective Nolan is working on a theory that Royce was meeting someone up there."

"Have they looked at his cell phone or email?"

"They're working on it. I take it you've decided to investigate?"

Sadie sighed. "I'm trying not to. But it is curious, what Amos said."

"Mmmhmm."

"And I do feel connected, finding the body and seeing Royce get in that fight earlier in the day. Do you know if they're looking at Jerry as a suspect?"

"He has an alibi. He stayed with his cousin in town overnight after getting out on bail."

"Could his cousin just be covering for him?"

"I guess."

"Have you heard a cause of death for Royce yet?"

"Not yet. Autopsy results are pending."

Sadie's phone buzzed in her pocket, and she took it out. She had a text from Jake.

`Bonfire tomorrow night at poplar. 7pm. Memorial for Royce.`

She showed the text to Penny.

"Better put on your deerstalker, Ms. Holmes. Looks like you have a date to sleuth the prime suspects. Now, can we order pizza to go with this wine? I'm starving."

# Chapter Nine

The first candidate Sadie saw for the barista position would not work out. It seemed by mutual agreement, and Sadie never expected to hear from the woman again. She didn't enjoy getting up early. Being in the coffee or bakery business meant getting up early.

The next candidate was ten minutes late. Sadie sat in the community room at the market and waited. And waited. When they finally showed, they didn't apologize for being late and asked what Sadie's policy on recreational cannabis was before she'd asked any questions. Sadie's policy was that she didn't care as long it didn't affect the job, but this candidate wouldn't get a chance to find that out.

The third candidate was promising. Luke was in his early twenties, had a permanent sunglasses tan, lived in Hoback Junction, and was a raft guide in the summer. He'd hurt his knee skiing, so he wouldn't be living out his dreams of shredding the slopes all winter and needed a job. He'd be fine if he could sit on a stool now and then and work around his physical therapy schedule, which Sadie could accommodate. Sadie sent him over to the coffee kiosk to get a tour and told him to ask Kendall for hiring paperwork if he wanted to work for them.

The fourth candidate didn't even show.

The fifth, Mirabel, a late-twenties Hispanic woman who fronted a local band, was also local to the Junction. Her availability was slimmer around gigs and band practices, but Sadie thought it could work out. She sent her out for the tour, too.

The last interview was with Holly Richards.

"Holly," Sadie said warmly as she approached her table. "I'm Sadie Moose. I've waved at you at Poplar, but never said hi."

Holly smiled back, flipping her shiny blonde hair over her shoulder before shaking her hand and sitting across from her.

"Yes, hello, so nice to finally say hi in person. I'm always chasing after our little monster when I see you, so it's hard to come over."

"She's adorable, by the way."

Holly laughed. "Thank you. She is, and she's a handful."

"Thanks for applying! I see you have barista experience." Holly detailed the experience Sadie had seen on her resume, all of which came before she'd had their two-year-old, Violet.

"I've been home with Violet since she was born. We moved here when she was six months, so it's been a bit of a whirlwind. But Cole is home all winter now, and I'd like to get back to work. And when he goes back to work, DeeDee, down at Poplar, said she could watch Violet for me part-time."

"Oh, that's nice." Sadie knew DeeDee. Her husband was an archaeologist for the Forest Service and she had three kids of her own, two of which were school-aged. Sadie went through her few interview questions, and Holly did great.

"We'd love to have you join us," Sadie said at the end of the interview. "I think you'd be a great fit! Everyone's coming on at the same barista level to start, but there will be an opportunity to move into the site manager role over time, if that's something that would interest you."

"It would," Holly confirmed. She grinned. "I'm so excited! It'll be good to be have something outside the home again. Sometimes I go days with no one talking to me except a two-year-old, and I'm sick of talking about Daniel Tiger and Elsa."

Sadie grimaced. "Well, Kendall loves Elsa and has a whole fan theory on her future storyline, so you might not get too far away from that," she laughed.

"Oh, I have theories, too!" Holly joked.

Sadie stood, and Holly did too.

"I'll walk you over to the kiosk so you can get a tour and we'll pick up the hiring paperwork." They left the market together, pulling on coats and gloves and hats as they did. The sky was blue, and it was below freezing.

"How is everyone doing down at Poplar?" Sadie asked as they crossed the parking lot.

Holly sighed. "It's tough. Royce was a larger-than-life figure in the neighborhood, and the loss is felt heavily by everyone."

Sadie made a murmuring sound of encouragement, and Holly continued.

"And we're all just so worried about what happened, and who could've done it. And that they're still out there! I'm barely sleeping. Not that I sleep much at all with a two-year-old, but still."

"That sounds rough." Sadie took a big step over an icy pothole.

"And I feel so bad for Cole. He didn't care for Royce much, but to be involved with the thing with Jerry, and then to have been in the area right before it happened…he's just beside himself thinking he could have stopped it had he been in the right place at the right time."

Sadie stopped, and Holly stopped to, turning to look at her curiously.

"I thought I saw Cole on the way up there," Sadie said. "So he wasn't at the hot springs?"

"No," Holly said, shaking her head. She put her hand up to shield her eyes from the sun to see Sadie better. "The trail keeps going past the hot springs, and there's a private inholding up there. Cole watches after the house for the owner in the winter for a stipend. He'd gone up to shovel the snow off the roofs before the next big dump came."

Sadie released a breath she hadn't known she'd been holding. That explained why Cole had been coming down so much later than everyone else, but hadn't been seen by Amos.

"You seem relieved," Holly said warily. "Why?"

"I was worried the cops might look at him since he was in the area and had been involved with Jerry that morning. Jake thinks so highly of Cole, you know. I don't know him, or you, well, but I was worried about all of you."

Holly gave a small smile. "Thanks for that. I'm excited to get to know you better. We'll have to do a double date night. Well. You'll have to come over for dinner after Violet goes to bed. That's about as good of a date night as we ever get anymore."

That sounded great to Sadie. She'd put it on her list of things to do. After she found the murderer in the neighborhood.

* * *

After the interviews and tours were over and the kiosk was closed, Sadie and Kendall sat down to make a training schedule. By splitting their days over the next two weeks, they'd be able to each train everyone twice, and hopefully handover kiosk operations to the new crew in the third week.

"And then what?" Kendall asked as she took a picture of the schedule and texted it to the new employees.

Sadie shrugged. "We go back to normal, I guess?"

Kendall didn't say anything, and Sadie frowned. It wasn't like her to not have something to say. She looked up at her. She was chewing her lip nervously.

"Unless you have a different idea?" Sadie felt uneasy. Was this when she found out Kendall was moving on to something else? She wasn't ready.

"Well..." Kendall started. She pulled out her phone and opened an app, typing something in and waiting for it to load. She turned the screen around and showed it to Sadie, who squinted at it, then took the phone from Kendall to look at it more closely.

It was a satellite map of a parking lot in Wilson along Wyoming Highway 22, west of Jackson. Sadie scrunched her nose and looked at Kendall questioningly.

"I was thinking...you should open another kiosk."

Sadie blinked at her.

"The building on this lot is recently vacated, and it's perfect easy access on and off the highway. Put a drive-thru kiosk there to catch all the commuters that come up over Teton Pass and Wilson, too? Plus traffic up to the big resort? You'd make a killing."

"You...are completely correct." Sadie zoomed in on the parking lot and the building, her mind whirling. She looked up at Kendall. "I'd need funding. I can't finance it myself."

Kendall nodded. "I know. But I would run it for you. Starting this up..." she looked around the kiosk, then grinned. "It's the most excited I've been about something in a while."

Sadie pursed her lips. "Where after that?"

"Alpine." Alpine was at the other side of the Snake River Canyon, a windy forty-minute drive from Hoback Junction. It was booming as a bedroom community to Jackson, with housing prices still within reach, if barely, of a two-income family.

Kendall grabbed her phone and pulled up a new location. She held it up to Sadie's face. "There's that new grocery store on the corner of the highway junction down in Alpine. You'd catch both way traffic."

Sadie blinked. When she took over the kiosk in Hoback Junction, she hadn't thought any further than that. She probably should have, but it was the first expansion Moose's Bakery had made in over forty years. She'd wanted to be careful, move slowly, protect the family legacy. But Kendall was right. It didn't take an MBA, which Sadie had, to figure out that with the first kiosk on course to be profitable before she'd expected, the market was hot for the service she was selling.

Sadie's only trepidation was profiting off the housing crisis that gripped her community by capitalizing off commuters. She firmly believed people should be able to live where they work. But a local business seizing the opportunity would employ local people and keep local dollars local. She could get the financing. She could open more locations. And, she could bring Kendall on in a more official role, keeping her close for longer. With a sudden rush of feeling that she was doing the right thing, she took a deep breath and dove in.

"I probably could negotiate something, but I think you'd do a better job."

"Be serious, Moose."

"I am being serious, Kendall. You're right, about more locations. I needed you to push me there. Maybe we should talk about you being more of a partner if we're going to move forward."

Kendall was never speechless. But in this moment, she was. For a moment, at least. Then she was asking Sadie to hold her phone so she could make a TikTok of this moment, and Sadie was laughing, and Kendall was admonishing her for jiggling the phone. When Kendall was done, they locked up with a promise to talk more formally in a few days. Sadie needed to go over the books again. To open two more kiosks, she'd need financing. To bring Kendall on as a partner, she'd need financing and a whole heck of legal help. But it felt right, and Sadie usually acted with her gut. Kendall turned up the highway towards Jackson to head home. Sadie turned the other way, headed south into the canyon to Poplar, where her gut was telling her something was very very wrong.

# Chapter Ten

Poplar was arranged on a circular drive, with a large grassy area, now covered with snow, in the middle. The open area held a community garden, playground, and some picnic tables. It was the community gathering place, and tonight, someone had drug a fire pit over from one of the houses and laid it high with wood for a bonfire. The community was gathering in honor of Royce, their unofficial mayor, who may have been a pain in the ass, but he was their pain in the ass.

The gathering was to begin at full dark, so Jake and Sadie hung out inside staying warm while dusk fell. Jake's house was an older stick-built house that had been erected at the Palisades Dam, about fifty miles away, in Idaho in the 1950s. Sometime in the 1980s, the federal agency that operated the dam had down-sized their employee housing and the Forest Service had moved half a dozen houses to their own housing site at Poplar. Sadie thought about the houses traveling along the dam, then making the turn to travel up the Snake River Canyon, and it seemed like such a feat. So much work.

In the last ten years, the insides of the houses had been completely ripped out, and they'd remodeled, so the insides had modern vinyl plank floors, cabinetry, and appliances. The rooms all had baseboard heat, but everyone relied on wood stoves to heat the houses. Jake's house was a three bedroom and one bathroom, with a large, rectangular open kitchen, dining, and living room, and a back entry with a pantry and laundry room off the kitchen. One hall ran down the middle of the house with bedrooms off each side and a bathroom at the end of the hall. It was simple, but comfortable, and cozy with the wood stove roaring and snow piled up as high as the windows.

They sat on the couch in Jake's living room, looking out one of the big plate-glass windows that overlooked the community area. Snow was piled halfway up the window from sliding off the roof. Sadie sipped a local IPA, and Jake had a cup of tea. He had to groom after the memorial, but Sadie was staying over.

"Explain to me again about the different lease agreements," Sadie said. Something was tickling her brain about the housing, and she couldn't remember what it was.

"Right. So these old dam houses–" Sadie smirked at him and he winked at her, "are owned by the Forest Service, and employees can rent them from the agency for three years, sometimes a fourth if they ask nicely, and then they have to move out. But there's agency-owned tiny homes in that secondary circle, and there's no time limit on those leases. The mobile homes are all on agency-owned trailer pads, but they're owned by the employees that live in them. They can stay as long as they're employed by the Forest here. If they retire or move, they can either take their house with them, or they can sell it to another employee."

"So complicated."

"Yep. And Royce was in an owned mobile home..."

Sadie perked up. That's what her brain had been getting around to. "Oooh, so his house is going to be sold?"

"It will go up for auction, I'm guessing. Royce had an ex-wife and a teenage kid he hadn't seen in a decade living some-where in Montana, so I imagine they'll get the proceeds."

Sadie finished her beer and stared out into the rapidly dark-ening sky. The reflection from inside was starting to be more visible than the outside.

"I know that look, Sadie Louise Moose," Jake grinned, putting his mug down and turning to pull her into his arms. "You're trying to solve a mystery." He kissed her cheek, then her nose, and then her lips, and Sadie giggled.

"I might be," she admitted. Jake kissed her then, and she didn't think about it for another minute, getting swept up in the fresh cut pine and wood smoke scent of him, the rasp of his beard, the wicked way his tongue stroked against hers. Jake was an amazing kisser.

When he finally pulled away, Sadie was breathless, but he was serious. "I don't want to think about any of my neighbors that way. I'm new here, but everyone's been so kind. Except for Royce, and, well…he's dead."

"Well, don't think about them that way then." Sadie patted his cheek, then gave him a nudge and he let go of her. She got up and peered out the window on the front door. It looked like her suspects were gathering. "I'll think it for you."

In the kitchen, she picked up a glass to fill with water, but Jake stopped her. "Oh, don't drink the tap water," he said. Sadie dumped her glass out.

"Oh?"

"It just tastes bad. I have jugs in the fridge, drink out of that."

"It's safe, though?"

Jake shrugged. "They say it is, they test it monthly. But it tastes bad, so most of us either filter it or just drink bottled."

Sadie filled a fresh glass with the jug from the fridge.

"They just lit the fire," Jake said then. "Let's go."

* * *

There didn't seem to be a program for the memorial. People showed up over time, and everyone stood in a circle, pondering the flames. There were about twenty people present. Sadie looked at each of their faces, trying to place everyone in the houses in the circle.

Jake was in house one, at the entrance of the circle. Next to him in house two were Cole, Holly, and Violet. They were there, bundled up in matching black North Face puffy coats, arms wrapped around each other's waists. Violet was probably in bed already. House three was the residence of Meadow Lin, a wildlife technician in her early thirties who kept to herself and was often away visiting her boyfriend, who lived several hours away. In house four was Officer Elaina. In house five was Darnell Bell, a recreation manager who ran the river patrol, and his wife, Tamia, an elementary school teacher. In house six, the final stick-built house, were three roommates, all seasonal employees that worked six months out of the year for the Forest Service in their regular jobs, then filled in where needed in the intervening months to pay their rent, like Jake was doing. Sadie had never caught their names, but they were all in their mid-twenties and stuck together. From what Jake had told her, their housing was expiring in the spring, and they weren't happy about it.

In the trailers was Jerry, of the fight with Royce, who was not there, then Carl Brent, the widower Paige had mentioned, and Justin and DeeDee Cox, along with their three kids. The fourth trailer had been Royce's. There were a few more people present, and Sadie guessed they lived in the tiny houses in the secondary, smaller circle behind the main circle, or were other coworkers of Royce's that didn't live there.

It was silent for a long time, people watching the flames

flicker and listening to the pop of sap igniting and exploding as sparks drifted into the clear winter sky. Finally, though, Elaina spoke.

"Royce was the first person I met here. I imagine that's true for a lot of us."

There were nods around the bonfire, shadowed faces looking around intently.

"I started in February, in the middle of a stretch that didn't get over zero for a week. He'd started the fire at my house and left a big load of wood, and turned on the baseboards in the bedrooms. That was kind. He didn't have to do that."

Jake stiffened at the mention of wood. Royce hadn't done that for him. He'd made Jake pay a premium and haul and stack the wood himself so he could get through his first winter here.

"He did the same for me," Meadow Lin said, her voice quiet. She had warm beige skin and angular eyes. "It was kind of him."

"He made great chili," DeeDee said, her voice wavering. Justin, a burly white man with a salt and pepper beard and bushy eyebrows, wrapped his arm around her shoulders, pulling her body into his. "It was so hot it made me cry, but I loved it," she finished with a whisper, wiping her eyes.

There were a few laughs then.

"He always pulled us the fastest on our sleds," the oldest of Justin and DeeDee's boys, Kayden, said, and the two younger boys, Karsen and Kyler, nodded soberly. "Everyone else worried about helmets and speed, but he didn't. He just hooked us up to the snowmobile and told us to hold on tight!"

There were groans and a few laughs.

The anecdotes piled up then.

"He always put up Christmas lights, even though there was just us to see them."

"He helped pull my car out of a ditch once and only yelled a little bit."

"He shoveled my porch when my back was out."

"He mowed my grass when Cole was out on fires all summer," Holly added.

After a while, the anecdotes slowed. The mood around the fire was relaxed, buoyed by good humor and memories.

Sadie could tell when the mood shifted and realized it was because a newcomer had joined them. It was Jerry, his craggy face still marred by yellowing bruises from the fight on Friday. The light of the bonfire cast him half in shadow, and he looked downright ghoulish. Sadie held her breath as everyone looked at him, waiting for him to speak.

"Royce Hensley was an asshole." Everyone gasped. "He stuck his nose in everyone's business, acted like he was the boss when he wasn't, and made threats to the livelihood and shelter of everyone around this fire. One of us probably killed him." There were shocked cries. "That said, he was a good fisherman. He was always in a shit mood when we went. But I'm grateful to him for showing me his favorite fishing spots, and I'll think of the bastard whenever I catch a rainbow trout."

There was a stunned silence, and then whispers as people looked around at each other suspiciously. Sadie perked her ears up, hoping to hear some gossip, but she didn't. Finally, the party seemed to break up.

"I'll stay and put out the fire," Cole volunteered.

"I can help," Jake said, but Cole shook his head.

"No, I want to do it alone."

Jake looked at Cole for a long moment, but finally shrugged, and Sadie, Jake, and Holly started across the circle to their houses. When they'd moved away from the fire, Holly whistled through her teeth.

"Jerry wasn't afraid to say the quiet part out loud, was he?"

"No," Sadie said. "Yikes."

"I hate to think he's right," Jake said, frowning. "I'm too new here to know all the backstory. Do you know what was between Jerry and Royce, Holly?"

Holly was silent a long moment, the only sound their boots crunching and squeaking in the snow as they tromped. Finally, she said, "Jerry was using his firewood processor to sell firewood as a side gig. It's not technically against the rules, but it walks a line between his work as a forester living in Forest Service housing and running a firewood business using trees from the Forest, even permitted cuttings, out of his backyard. Royce told the Ranger about it and Jerry had to go in and justify his business to her."

That explained why Jerry had kept telling Royce it wasn't his business the morning of the fight.

"Did the Ranger tell him he had to quit?" Sadie asked.

"I don't think she'd decided yet, before all this. But Royce had Jerry all spun up that he was going to get kicked out of Poplar because of it."

They walked in silence for another minute, coming to a stop in front of their houses. Sadie looked up and took in the stars, and her two companions did the same. It was a clear, bitterly cold night, and Sadie missed the heat of the bonfire. But the stars were brilliant, the moon waning but still casting a blue light over everything. It reminded her of the night they'd found Royce. She counted back, realizing that was only three nights ago, and shivered.

"I had nothing against Royce," Holly said suddenly. "Cole didn't like him, but they got along for the good of the neighborhood. Cole was on the trail that night, but he didn't kill him."

Sadie dropped her head from the stars to study Holly. She wore a blue knit hat low over her ears, her long blonde braid peeking out the back. Her cheeks were ruddy from the cold.

Her eyes were a clear blue, and they looked straight at her. She was sincere.

"Did Cole see anything?"

"He said he didn't. But you should ask him, Sadie. You're looking into things. Ask everyone. The police detective has been out here to ask questions, but they don't seem like they're getting anywhere. Thinking that the killer could be one of my neighbors is driving me crazy. Maybe you'll figure it out. People will be more likely to talk to you anyway, I bet."

Jake wrapped an arm around Sadie's ample waist and pulled her into his body. "I don't like the idea of either of you being in danger." His voice was low and protective.

"I have Cole to look after me," Holly assured him. "And he'll watch your house if you're gone and Sadie's there."

"I'll ask around," Sadie said finally. "It should be pretty simple to find out what people were doing that night." Jake's arm tightened around her and she looked up at him. His look showed concern, and she smiled at him. "I'll be careful, I promise."

# Chapter Eleven

Jake's house was a little creepy at night.

At first it had been kind of fun, being there alone. She'd sent Jake off with a kiss, and he'd walked out the door with his lunchbox, headphones, and winter gear, promising to try not to wake her when he came home.

First she'd helped herself to ice cream from his freezer, walking around peering at things without really snooping as she ate it. She'd never been here alone. And she'd only been into the bedroom to crash Friday night. One room was his bedroom, one was setup as an office, and the third was full of boxes he hadn't opened from his move. Not much to see there. When she'd gotten bored peering into closets—to be honest, Jake wasn't a man of much intrigue—she fed another log into the fire, then settled onto the couch to watch something on Netflix. She'd turned on the TV when she realized the blinds were still open, and anyone could see her from outside. That was the first pang of discomfort she'd had. She'd quickly closed all the blinds, made sure the doors were locked, and put her phone on her lap as she crawled back under the blanket on the couch.

She missed Tyrone, so she FaceTimed Kamari, who was on Tyrone-sitting duty. Kamari answered with a yawn.

"Girl, it's late," she complained. She adjusted her bonnet and frowned into the camera.

"It's nine-thirty and you're almost a decade younger than me," Sadie protested.

"Yeah, but I have training at five, then have to be up at Snow King by nine, and then my bitch of a boss at the bakery expects me in by eleven." Kamari was an up and coming freeride snowboarding star trying to compete her way onto the competitive circuit. Free ride was open mountain snowboarding, no parks or manufactured pipes. She coached the local junior freeride team when she wasn't training or working at Moose's to cover her bills.

Sadie groaned. "That schedule is brutal. Don't come in, I'll cover you tomorrow."

"I didn't ask for help," Kamari said bluntly. "I'll do it. But I need my beauty rest to not snap at the customers."

"And I'll let you get it if I can see my little moosey baby." Kamari rolled her eyes but turned the camera around to reveal Tyrone laying next to her in bed.

"He's not allowed on furniture," Sadie laughed.

"What his mama doesn't know won't hurt him," Kamari crooned from behind the camera, reaching her elegant umber-toned hand into the frame to scratch the blissed out dog's ears.

"I'll pretend I don't know then," Sadie conceded. "I miss you, Ty. Sleep well. Thanks for watching him for me, Kamari."

Kamari flipped the camera back around. "Anytime. You find anything good snooping around down there?"

Sadie snorted. "I didn't snoop."

"Mmhmm, I bet," she said knowingly. "Though Jake doesn't seem like much of a man of mystery."

Sadie bristled, though she realized she'd thought the same thing earlier. "He has depths, Kamari."

Kamari narrowed her eyes at her. "I didn't say he didn't, you did. Anyway. Is it spooky down there?"

"No," Sadie lied.

"You're a terrible liar, Moose. I'm going to bed. Lock the doors," Kamari said. And she hung up.

Sadie was glad Tyrone was having a good night with Kamari, but she missed him. Almost everyone in Poplar had a dog, and she had a feeling Tyrone would be a happy member of the pack if he could roam with them. But it was so cold during the day, he couldn't hang out in her Subaru, and there was no room for him in the coffee kiosk. Sadie decided the next time she came down to work intending to stay with Jake overnight, she'd just leave early and bring him down here, then double back to the kiosk. The extra ten minutes would be worth having him for company.

When she got bored with the newest hard-bodies-stuck-on-an-island-making-out reality show she'd tuned into, she got ready for bed. She filled the wood stove as full of wood as she could so it would stay warm, then washed her face and teeth and climbed into Jake's bed. For a bachelor, he had an excellent bed. It was a firm memory foam mattress with quality soft cotton sheets and blankets. He even had a throw pillow. She looked over at his side of the bed and smiled as she turned out the light. There was a stack of books—mostly submarine spy novels—a pair of reading glasses, a water bottle, and a bottle of tums. Except for the lack of ski magazines, it looked like her dad's bedside table, and it made her feel warm inside. Despite his dangerous career and nomadic summers, Jake was a solid, comforting man. He wasn't an enigma, and sometimes she wondered at the depths behind his sunny disposition, but she was glad they were exploring what this was, and what it could be.

She plugged her smartphone into the cord he'd thoughtfully put on her side of the bed and turned on white noise in her meditation app. Soothing rain sounds were her favorite, and would keep her from waking with every pop of the fire and creak of the house. She lay her head down on the pillow. He had squishy or memory foam options. What a dream man! She shut her eyes, purposely not thinking of a blonde man of mystery from her past, the murder at the hot springs, or that she was falling asleep surrounded by suspects.

* * *

When Sadie jolted awake, she lay still, trying to decide what had woken her. She couldn't hear anything over the white noise app, so she grappled for her phone in the dark, swiping it on and pausing the sound. Her lock screen said it was 2:17 a.m. She'd been asleep about three hours. It was a little early for Jake to be home. So what had woken her? Her breaths seemed loud in the suddenly quiet house and she fought to steady them. Just when she'd decided she was being silly, she heard a sharp rap on the front door and jumped.

Who would knock this early? Sudden, icy fear gripped her heart. Had something happened to Jake? She checked her phone again. She didn't see any calls or texts. The knock came again. She peered at her phone closer and realized that not only did she have no cell service, which was normal at Poplar, but she also didn't have any Wi-Fi, which they relied on for calling out. Panic gripped her. What was she supposed to do? She couldn't call anyone if the person at the door was an axe murderer!

*Axe murderers don't knock, though,* Sadie thought, and she let out a short laugh. She climbed out of bed and cautiously made her way down the hall to the living room. The wood stove cast light on the walls in strange patterns, and Sadie steeled herself, not willing to let herself spook anymore. There had been no noise from the door in a moment, and she told herself whoever it had been was probably gone. The front door had a window on the top half, and an in-window blind that was down. To look out it, Sadie would have to push the lever to open the blind, revealing herself to whoever was on the other side. She cast about the room wildly for a weapon, her eyes coming to rest on the tools leaning neatly beside the wood stove. The blow poke, a wicked long cast iron tube used for poking the fire on one end and blowing to fan the flames on the other caught her eye, and she grabbed it.

She took a deep breath and slowly cracked the blind.

No one was there. She flipped on the porch light and opened the blind all the way. The light shone brightly on the front porch and just beyond, illuminating Sadie's car and the space where Jake normally parked. She didn't see any movement, and no other lights were on in the circle. Had she imagined it? She took a step back from the door, relaxing her shoulders.

*Knock knock knock!*

Sadie jumped. This time, the sound came from the back door. Heart in her throat, Sadie crept through the kitchen and into the mudroom. This was a whole door, no window to peep out of.

"Who's...who's there?" She asked, her voice faint and distant to her own ears.

"Sadie? It's me. Let me in, honey."

The breath Sadie had been holding whooshed out of her at the sound of Jake's voice. With shaky hands, she undid the deadbolt and door lock and opened the door a crack, blow poke still in her other hand. Jake's face, pale and cold, his beard covered in frost but still smiling, greeted her and she let him in.

"What happened?" She asked as he came in, dropping his backpack and shivering. He was covered in snow, like he'd been walking a long way.

"I locked my damn keys in the truck," he said sheepishly. "I'm going to grab my extra set and walk back over and get it now. Storm's coming in, and I don't want it to get stuck over there."

"Do you want me to drive you?" Her heart was finally beating normally.

"No, babe, you go back to bed. I'm so sorry I had to wake you." He glanced down at the blow poke in her hand. "Nice choice of weapon." He pressed a kiss to her forehead and moved around her into the kitchen to dig around in the junk drawer. "There's a baseball bat under my side of the bed for next time."

"No handgun in the bedside table?" She asked weakly.

Jake found the keys and looked up at her. "I keep everything locked up in my gun safe. The Cox kids have been known to show up in your house when you least expect it, so I don't keep anything unsecured. Do you know how to use a handgun?"

Sadie blinked at him. "I was joking."

"I have rifles for hunting and a handgun I take with me when I'm camping. I'm no gun nut though."

Sadie knew he wasn't. There wasn't an NRA sticker on the back of his pickup. But this was Wyoming, after all. Most people Sadie knew owned guns, and most of the men and a few of the women she knew hunted.

"Hey, are you okay?" Jake asked, coming towards her. He laid a cold hand on her cheek. "I'm sorry I scared you. I was trying to figure out how to do this without freaking you out, but the Wi-Fi is out again so I couldn't text or call you."

"I was a little freaked," Sadie admitted. "Hence the blow poke. But yeah, I'm okay."

Jake kissed her then, a light one because his beard was wet with frost, and gently pushed her into the kitchen. "Go get back in bed. I'm going to go get my rig, then come back and shower and climb in with you."

Sadie replaced her makeshift weapon and adjusted the damper on the wood stove, then went back to bed. Before she crawled in, she reached under Jake's side and fished the baseball bat out from underneath and put it under her side instead. She checked her phone again. 2:30 a.m., and the Wi-Fi was still out. She turned her white noise on and laid her head down, but it was a long time, even after Jake had come back in and showered and crawled in next to her, pulling her up against him as he instantly fell asleep, before her mind drifted off.

But in the morning, when Sadie went out to dust an inch of fine, powdery snow off her Subaru, she noticed footprints had walked around her car. Large, booted prints, circling it, stopping, and then circling back. It hadn't been snowing when Jake had come home. Who had it been? And why?

# Chapter Twelve

Sadie had wondered how she would question the residents of Poplar, but she shouldn't have worried. Throughout the morning, they came through her line at the coffee kiosk and offered to answer the questions she had, apparently tipped off by Holly that Sadie was investigating. Sadie had to keep their interviews short so she didn't rile up the caffeine seekers behind them, but by mid-morning, she had a better idea of what the residents of Poplar had been up to the night Royce was murdered.

First through her line was DeeDee Cox. DeeDee was in her mid-forties, a plump white brassy blonde with a heavy hand with makeup. She drove her beat-up minivan through the line after dropping her oldest two off at the bus stop just south of the market. The kids bussed in to Jackson for school. Her youngest, a giggly four-year-old with a bowl cut named Kyler, was jabbing at a tablet in the backseat while DeeDee ordered a toasted marshmallow latte with whipped cream and two double chocolate muffins, one for her, and one for Kyler.

"Justin and I have lived here since before our oldest was

born. The only person who had been at Poplar longer than us was Royce. We had our problems over the years, but as the oldest residents and permanent ones, we were a united front on housing issues, and on keeping the neighborhood character intact."

Sadie wondered what that meant. In Jackson, residents used that to mean they didn't want any affordable, multi-family housing in their backyards, even if they agreed that more housing was needed in the valley.

"Had you had any disagreements lately?"

DeeDee averted her heavily blue-eye-shadowed eyes, then looked back at Sadie.

"No."

"Where were you on Friday night?"

DeeDee laughed. "At home with the kids! We don't get out much anymore. We had a family game night and the kids went to bed around nine. Justin turned in around ten. I stayed up to work on my business. So I saw the deputies arrive and them and Elaina take off toward the parking area with their snowmobiles loaded up and knew something was going on. I woke Justin up, and it wasn't long after that we heard what happened."

Sadie handed DeeDee her coffee and muffins and held out the iPad for her to pay.

"Do you know anyone else in the neighborhood that had fought with Royce lately?"

"Besides Jerry? Well, the three kids in number six had words with him last week about their housing extension request being denied. And I saw him over on Meadow's porch last week, and could hear her voice raised while she talked to him. I thought it was odd, considering Meadow rarely talks to any of us."

Deedee left, with the promise to get in contact with Sadie if she thought of anything relevant to the crime. As she drove away, Sadie noticed the decal on her back window advertising "Elegant Expressions by DeeDee", including a Facebook and Instagram handle. Apparently, DeeDee had a side hustle.

"This one's yours," Kendall said behind her.

"How do you know that?" Luke asked. It was his first day of training, and so far he'd been a quick study.

"It's a murder suspect," Kendall shrugged. Luke looked at Sadie with wide eyes and she tried to laugh it off as they switched windows.

"What murder?" She heard Luke hiss at Kendall as they took the next customer's order.

Sadie slid the window open to find Darnell Bell in a gray SUV waiting for her. Darnell was a handsome, tall, wide-shoul-dered man with warm brown eyes and a wide smile.

"Good morning," Sadie said. "Headed back to Poplar?"

"Working from home today, but I wanted to stop by for a coffee and answer any questions you had." His voice was deep and rich.

Sadie worked on his coffee order while they talked. "Did you have any issues with Royce?"

"Royce wasn't an easy man to get along with. When we first moved into the neighborhood, he didn't make us feel very welcome. I can't say it's because we're Black, but we definitely look different from everyone else down there. Our first year in the house, we had an issue with the plumbing and I kept asking to get it fixed and Royce kept putting it off. Eventually I went over his head, and that made him mad, but the work got done. After that, whenever we needed something, he did it for us."

"Anything recent?"

Darnell sighed. "Our shed has been in bad shape. Last week I realized it had been leaking inside. Some boxes we didn't have room to unpack were ruined. Tamia was pretty upset. Some things aren't replaceable. We'd mentioned that we needed a repaired or new shed last year, and nothing had happened. Tamia got upset with Royce, but it blew through fast. There was nothing to be done about what had already happened, and Royce tried to fix the worst of the leaks to get us through winter."

"Where were you Friday night?"

"At the movies. Saw the new one with that guy from Star Wars all the women like..." he raised his eyebrows at her, and Sadie laughed.

"Adam Driver?"

"Yeah. Funny looking dude in my opinion. We had dinner at Carloni's, then saw the late show, so we weren't back to the house until after Elaina had ridden up to the hot springs. We followed several deputies from town, and Tamia was worried. When we got home, DeeDee told us what had happened."

"Anyone else have trouble with Royce recently?"

"Besides Jerry?"

"Yeah. Well...DeeDee runs one of those home-based businesses with parties and stuff? I think they're a scam, but Tamia buys makeup from her. Since Royce had been on Jerry about his firewood business, I wonder if he had a problem with DeeDee's business? I saw the two of them going at it a couple weeks ago."

Interesting. DeeDee hadn't mentioned that. Sadie sent Darnell on his way with his coffee and a ham and cheese croissant, then took the next few orders before turning the window over to Luke, who Kendall had deemed ready to run a window.

"Shit!" She heard Kendall say over the pumping K-pop playlist, and she turned to see her digging around in the refrigerator.

"What'd we run out of?"

"Whole milk, unbelievably." Kendall pulled her head out of the fridge. "Want me to run over to the market?"

"I'll do it. You two have this handled, anyway." Sadie pulled on her coat and slipped out the back door, darting through two waiting cars with a wave, and then carefully picked her way across the icy parking lot.

Slowly, Sadie realized a vehicle was driving behind her, and she moved closer to the parked row of cars to get out of the way. Still, the car drove slowly. She glanced over her shoulder to see a man in a white truck with the Forest Service shield on the door. He gave her a two-finger steering wheel wave. She stopped, and he pulled alongside. Sadie peered in. It was Carl Brent. He was a white man with graying hair and a sullen expression.

"Didn't mean to startle you," he said in a relaxed, even voice.

"Oh, it's okay." Sadie waved it off.

"Holly told me to come by and talk to you."

"I appreciate that. How are you doing, Carl?"

He averted his eyes and took a quick breath. After a pause, he looked back at her, his brown eyes somber. "I'm not great, Ms. Moose. But thank you for asking."

"I was very sorry to hear about the loss of your wife."

"I appreciate that. And thank you for donating the baked goods at her fundraiser."

"The least I could do. Holly asked me to ask around about Royce. Do you mind if I ask if you had any trouble with him?"

"I didn't."

Sadie paused. That was a first.

"Oh. Were the two of you friends?"

"No."

"Do you know of anyone who did have trouble with him?"

"Most people did. I didn't let him bother me, though."

"How long have you been at Poplar?"

"Six years."

"Can I ask where you were Friday night?"

"At home," he said smoothly. "Alone. But I was at home. DeeDee lives next door, she can attest to my truck never leaving that night."

*Not much information to share,* Sadie thought. "I appreciate you stopping to talk to me. Oh! And I saw you in the paper this weekend. What's it like to be close to wildlife like that?"

"Intimidating," he said, "but it's my life's work." He didn't crack a smile. Carl nodded at her, and she stepped back. He drove on, out of the parking lot, leaving her standing there thinking.

Was someone a better suspect if they didn't admit to a motive? Did that mean they were hiding something? Or was Carl just a quiet man grieving for his wife who kept to himself?

* * *

By the end of the day, the only people from Poplar Sadie hadn't talked to were the three roommates, Meadow, and any of the residents of the tiny homes. Their names were still a mystery. And Cole, but she'd talked to Holly, so that seemed almost close enough.

She left Kendall and Luke to close up and climbed into her Subaru. Before she could put her car into park, her phone buzzed in her pocket, and she pulled it out. She sighed heavily, but answered the call.

"Lilith?"

"Sadie!" The older woman's voice was panicked. "Amos got fired!"

"Oh, Lilith, I'm sorry." Sadie was genuinely sorry. "Did they say why?"

"He told me it was for drinking on the job, but I'm sure his test results are going to come back negative!"

"They're still not in? It's been five days!"

"Not yet. Tell me, please, that you've found something that could clear him? I'm so worried he's going to turn back into his old self, out drinking and carousing and getting into trouble..." Lilith trailed off with a muffled sob.

Sadie chewed on her nail as she thought about it. "There are lots of suspects other than Amos," Sadie said finally. "I talked to a bunch of Royce's neighbors today, and I'm about to go question more."

"Oh thank goodness," Lilith said. "Amos is coming to stay with me until you can get him cleared and we can get him his job back!"

Sadie frowned. "I don't want you to get too excited. I don't know that I'll solve this thing..."

"Of course you will, dear," Lilith said, her voice suddenly cheery. "We believe in you! I'm going to make up the guest bedroom. I wonder if he still likes those Poke-whatever-characters? The yellow one? I have a comforter from when he was a kid. And I'll put a pot of soup on."

Sadie assured her that Pokémon were all the rage again, then they exchanged goodbyes. She hoped Amos would accept the help he was being given, and stay on the path he'd put himself on despite these setbacks. She was hopeful. After all, being cozied up in a guest room with a cartoon comforter from childhood and Lilith Dormer's famous chicken noodle soup sounded like a good place to be.

Energized, Sadie pulled onto the highway heading towards Poplar instead of town. She entered the roundabout at the highway junction, proceeding south into Snake River Canyon. Homes lined both sides of the highway for a half mile, and then the road pulled above the river and left the houses behind. She went around a bend, slowing for a perpetually icy patch, and stayed slow through a frequent elk crossing. The canyon was still wide open here, and the road came back down into the river bed. She passed the red bridge that crossed the Snake River, leading to a new expensive development and the recently opened public Astoria Hot Springs pools. The road curved again, the river to her left and a wide meadow underneath mountains on her right. Elk congregated in the meadow, waiting for their daily feed delivered by game wardens. The meadow gave way to a thick stand of poplars and cottonwoods with scattered evergreens, and soon Sadie turned right onto the road that led to Poplar, and if you went past it, to Pritchard Hot Springs, where she'd found a dead body five days ago.

*And it leads to a private inholding, too.* Sadie had forgotten about that, and her mind grabbed onto it. She'd have to ask Jake if he'd ever been up there. How far from the hot springs was it? Who maintained that road? Did the landowners ever come back in the winter? How had Cole gotten that gig? Sadie wondered if the killer could have hidden up there while everyone came up the mountain, sneaking away later. But the main road had been closed and patrolled. How would they have missed someone leaving? Really, it made the most sense that Amos had done it. But Sadie believed him when he said he hadn't. What a conundrum.

Sadie considered that as she drove through the trees and past the authorized personnel only sign that led to the housing complex. There was just too much she didn't know yet. She didn't know the manner of Royce's death, or the time. Or why he'd been there that night. She didn't know what had happened to Amos, of if he was even telling the truth about being sober that night. There were too many holes for her to fit the pieces of the puzzle together. She needed some answers, perhaps from Penny or–

She pressed the brake to stop suddenly. A Jackson Hole Police Department SUV was parked across the road, blocking traffic. An officer was getting out of the vehicle at her approach, and Sadie recognized him as none other than Penny's "mistake" himself, Officer Greg Knott. She needed answers, and he would do.

# Chapter Thirteen

"Can't let you through, Ms. Moose," Officer Knott said as Sadie got out of her car to talk with him.

"Hello to you too, Officer," Sadie said, smiling charmingly.

"Oh yes, hello," he said, his cheeks reddening slightly.

"We haven't been formally introduced," Sadie smiled. "Call me Sadie, would you?"

Officer Knott blinked at her. "Fine. Can't let you through, Sadie."

"And can I call you Greg? You are, um—dating—one of my oldest friends, you know." At the word "dating", Officer Knott's face flushed, his normally ruddy cheeks turning even redder.

"I'm not sure you could call it dating," he said, a bitter edge to his voice. "Penny doesn't really let herself be dated."

"You're telling me," Sadie commiserated, leaning back up against her Subaru. "She's a tough nut to crack."

Officer Knott scoffed.

"Aw," Sadie said. "I can tell you really care about her. I appreciate that. She could use a little shaking up."

"You can call me Greg," he said finally. He glanced around. "As long as the detective isn't around."

"Deal."

"And if I can ask your advice about Penny."

Sadie frowned. "You can ask, but no guarantee I'll answer. My loyalty is always to my friend first."

"Fair."

"So, shoot." Sadie startled, her gaze snapping to the pistol on the officer's duty belt, then held up her hands. "I mean. Not shoot. But ask your question."

"At ease," Greg said, scoffing, and Sadie relaxed, grinning at him. "I know I'm not Penny's normal type. I want to meet her in the middle on her interests, but I'm not really into...rockabilly stuff, and I'm not musical like her last boyfriend. Do you have any ideas?"

Sadie pondered that, her gloved fingertip tapping against her lips. She looked Greg up and down. From his buzzed blonde hair to his shiny shoes, he looked wound tight. Finally, she snapped her fingers. "I got it! Maybe work on dressing in more vintage pieces? Asking for a snappy new style that still felt like you could be something to do together."

Greg frowned.

"I'm not suggesting you start dressing like Lyle Lovett. But you already like shiny shoes and creased dress pants, right? Your uniform is one step away from some sort of vintage look."

Greg seemed to take that in. "Okay. I'll think about it. I can look on Pinterest. Is that still a thing?"

"Oh, definitely," Sadie said. "You can lose hours there. Also try TikTok."

He winced. "I have to draw the line somewhere," he said, his voice stern again.

"So...now that I've helped you and we're friends..." Sadie's tone wheedled.

"Still can't let you through."

"Can you tell me why? Is everything okay?"

"They're executing a search warrant."

"Oooh," Sadie said. She stood up straighter and inched her way closer to the police SUV, peeking around the back end of it. She could just make out the housing complex through the trees, but she couldn't see any action.

"Which house?"

"I really shouldn't–"

"I'm going to find out pretty quick. My boyfriend Jake is home, so he'll just tell me when I talk to him."

"Jerry Givens."

Sadie's mouth formed an O, and she made wide eyes. "I thought he had an alibi!"

Greg shrugged at her, his lips tightly sealed.

"Huh. Say, Greg. Now that we're friends. How did Royce die?"

"C'mon, Sadie..."

"I'm sure you're going to release the information to the papers soon anyway, right? The people want to know. I just need a little preview."

"Why are you poking around in this, anyway?" Greg narrowed his eyes at her.

"Besides being the one to find the body? Amos Garner is a friend of a friend, and Holly Richards is so terrified she can't sleep at night. I'm just asking some questions."

"Detective Nolan has this well in hand."

Sadie harrumphed at that. There was silence for a moment.

"Was he pushed in? Hit his head on a rock? Held under and drowned?"

No response.

"Blink twice if I get it right."

Greg closed his eyes.

"You're no fun. Did someone knock him over the head with something? I keep trying to think about what someone could have found on the scene to use. A loose rock? They're all covered in snow, though. A tool of some sort?"

Greg's eyes were still closed. Sadie got the impression he was moments away from putting his hands over his ears to block out not just the sight of her, but the sound, too.

"Was he shot? Poisoned? Knifed? Run through with a sword? Oh, I got it!" Greg's eyes flew open at her exclamation.

"It was a pie server, wasn't it?"

He barked out a laugh, and Sadie grinned at him, and then her smile fell. She probably shouldn't joke about that. Slowly, Greg's smile fell, too.

He looked around, peeking over the top of the SUV to make sure they were alone. "Fine. He was hit in the head with an object which knocked him out, and then he fell in and drowned."

"An...object? Wanna play twenty questions? Was it bigger or smaller than a breadbox?"

"We don't know exactly what yet."

"Looking for it in Jerry's house, though, huh?"

Greg shrugged at her, then mimed zipping his lips and throwing away a key. That was the end of the information she was getting from him. But she'd made a new friend and found out the manner of Royce's death, as well as the police's number one suspect. Not a bad way to spend a few minutes.

"Do me a favor and don't tell the detective I was here, yeah?" Sadie climbed back into her car. "And thank you!" she yelled out the window, backing up to a wide spot in the road to turn around, careful not to slip off into a snowdrift. She'd have to talk to Meadow and the three roommates later.

* * *

Jake had one more night of grooming before he was off until the weekend, so Sadie stayed in Jackson. They made plans to get together the next night for dinner. As far as the search went, Jake had little to report. The officers had been there for several hours and had carried a few boxes and bags out. Then they'd left. He hadn't seen Jerry since the night of the bonfire, and he didn't know anything else.

Despite what Sadie had learned from the residents of Poplar and Officer Knott—Greg, she corrected—what had happened at the hot springs will still a mystery to her. And sitting at home staring at a blank notepad and thinking it through wasn't going to help. What she needed was to get out of the house, get some fresh air, and eat something more filling than what she could create from the paltry contents of her fridge. Sadie filled a dog treat ball with peanut butter and gave it to Tyrone with a pat on the head. Then she put on her winter layers and locked the door behind her, turning her feet toward the local brewpub.

It was only three blocks, and Sadie enjoyed the cold air, her breaths coming out in white puffs as she walked. The first block was in her neighborhood. She waved at Sarah O'Donnell as she drove by in her beat up SUV. Sarah was the matriarch of the large O'Donnell family, a stay-at-home mom in her mid-forties to seven kids from high school to elementary school. Her husband, Curtis, was an engineer for the Town of Jackson. They were currently building a Habitat for Humanity home, but weren't able to move in for six months. When the rent on their house had doubled, Sadie had happily leased them the house that had most recently belonged to Merritt but now, through Merritt's machinations, belonged to her. Sadie needed to figure out what she was going to do with the house long term. Renting at a rate that covered the utilities and property taxes to the O'Donnells had allowed her to make a difference in the lives of a local family, keep them local, and punt that decision down the road. It was fun to see activity in the house again, after it had sat empty for years. Plus, the older O'Donnell girls were great dog sitters, and the youngest ones worshipped her for always bringing them sugar cookies.

After she left her neighborhood, she walked past one block of quiet office buildings. The bottom floors were exclusively real estate or law offices. Sadie paused in front of one of the realtor's displays. Poster-sized listings were displayed on easels and spotlit for easy viewing. Not a single home was available for under $1.5 million, and most of them were over $3 million. She rolled her eyes and kept walking, hitting the boardwalk at the end of the block.

The next block was bustling with activity. A transit bus pulled to a stop ahead of her, and a group dressed for skiing piled out, their boots banging loudly on the boardwalk as they unloaded their skis from the exterior racks and turned towards their hotel lodgings, loudly calling back and forth about dinner plans. Restaurants and bars lined the street on both sides. Many restaurants still had covered outdoor seating areas, a product of the pandemic that had thankfully never gone away. They were strung prettily with lights and all had outdoor propane heaters burning to keep their diners warm. Guests wore parkas and fingerless gloves, and Sadie heard laughter, the scrape of cutlery, and the clinking of glasses as she strolled by.

One block back from the busy main road sat the brewpub. The sprawling two story building was industrial chic, all corrugated metal and exposed beams, with a giant still outside and windows that spanned both stories showing that they brewed onsite. There was a large courtyard with a fire pit and scattered seating. In the summer, the courtyard picnic tables were the hottest seating in town, offering easy access to the corn hole, giant chess, and yard Jenga games that were always setup. Now, everything was covered in two feet of snow. A crowd stood around the fire pit anyway, clutching pint glasses with the brewery's logo on them as they talked about the "wicked lines" they'd taken on the mountain that day.

Sadie stepped inside and stomped snow off her boots, unwinding the scarf from around her neck and pulling off her knit beanie. The bar area was busy, despite it being a Tuesday night in mid-January. It was the height of ski season, after all. Upstairs was the main dining area, and from the hub of activity around the hostess stand, Sadie guessed it was busy there too. Spotting her friend and head brewer Nash O'Conner behind the bar, Sadie headed that direction instead of grabbing a table.

Nash spotted her heading his way and grinned. He stepped back to survey the packed bar and waved her towards a just-emptying stool in the middle, close to the taps.

Sadie settled on the stool and smiled gratefully at Nash when she turned around to a fresh pint of her favorite IPA already in front of her.

"You know how to treat a lady," she said, taking a big gulp and sighing.

Nash winked at her. He was a tall, burly white man with shaggy red hair and a mountain man beard. He'd grown up in Jackson, a few years ahead of Sadie in school as part of the crowd of local kids that had grown up in her neighborhood, just like Penny and Paige. After college, he'd come back to town and started working as a brewer, eventually working his way up to head brewer at the pub. He still liked to work the bar, though, if only to keep up on the gossip that inevitably came his way.

"I wondered when you'd show up here." Nash eyed the bar, then seemingly satisfied he could check out for a minute, propped a hip on the bar and settled in for a chat. "Dish."

"Did you order–"

"Put it in the computer as soon as I saw you come in," Nash assured her, taking a drink of water from a glass he'd poured.

Satisfied she could soon shove perfectly fried logs of mozzarella cheese into her mouth, Sadie relented, telling Nash about what had happened at the hot springs and since. He made appropriate ooh and aww and "oh wow" sounds, leaving only twice to take care of customers. When Sadie finished, her beer was mostly gone and Nash was putting her plate of mozzarella sticks in front of her. The barstool next to Sadie opened, and Nash looked at his watch.

"Time for my break," he said, signaling to the other two bartenders he was taking a break by pouring his own pint and coming around the bar to sit next to Sadie. Once he was settled, he took a gulp of his own beer, then leaned in to talk to Sadie, his voice a low rumble.

"Ah!" Sadie exclaimed, interrupting him, fanning her mouth.

"They're always hot. Every time. You do this every time."

Sadie rolled her eyes at him and took a drink, cooling off her fiery mouth. He had a point. But it was worth it for the oh-so-gooey cheesiness.

"Listen, I didn't know Royce, but I know Jerry. He's a regular here, and our firewood supplier."

Sadie raised her eyebrows. "He doesn't seem like the craft beer type."

"It's Jackson. Everyone's a craft beer type, even if you drink Bud Light at home."

"What do you know about him?"

"He's always seemed like a nice guy. Hard worker. Fair prices for wood. Doesn't seem like the kind of guy to kill someone."

"Does he seem like the kind of guy to attack another guy in a public parking lot?"

Nash considered. "Nope."

"Then I don't know how well you can know him, because I saw him do just that."

"Guess you don't really know someone based on their beer order and how they stack firewood, then."

Sadie bit into another mozzarella stick and chewed, thinking. "Do you know Amos Garner?"

"Haven't seen him around this season, but yeah, he used to come in here with a group of resort lifties. Kicked him out for being too drunk to be served and rowdy at least once."

"Hmm."

"You got any hunches what happened up there?"

"I really don't. It's still a mystery. I have a few people to talk to still, but it seems like a lot of people had a reason to dislike Royce. Though none of the reasons seem enough to kill him?"

"Maybe the police will figure it out." Nash gave her a look.

"They're concentrating on Jerry and Amos."

"Not your most likely suspects?"

"Jerry has an alibi, and I believe Amos will be cleared when his test results eventually come back."

They were silent for a few minutes, the sound of loud conversation, bar glasses clinking together, and indistinguishable background music swallowing up their thoughts.

"I keep wondering why Royce was even up there. For a secret meeting? Who was he meeting? Why? How did that person get away if Royce died between the last thing Amos remembers and us arriving?"

"I know who he was meeting," said an unfamiliar voice behind them.

# Chapter Fourteen

Sadie whirled around on her barstool to confront the speaker, her eyes widening when she saw Meadow Lin standing there. Stunned to silence, Nash stepped in, introducing himself and getting up, offering Meadow his seat.

"Looks like you two need to talk. Get you anything?"

Meadow ordered a pale ale, and settled in next to Sadie. She looked at Sadie's plate.

"Uh...want a mozzarella stick?"

"I'm lactose intolerant. And yes." Sadie pushed the plate closer to her.

"I'm sorry you overheard me. I thought I was talking quietly."

"You were, I was being especially big-eared, though." Meadow took a nibble of her mozzarella stick, smiling at Nash as he put a pale ale down in front of her. He put a second beer in front of Sadie, then wandered down the bar. Meadow took a gulp, then sighed.

"I'm not involved in this at all. I was out of town visiting my boyfriend the night Royce died. I didn't kill him."

"Okay."

"But I saw him having an argument with someone, and I'm pretty sure that's who he was meeting with."

Sadie waited a beat. "Who was it, Meadow?"

"I don't know the person's name, but he came into the neighborhood and pulled up in front of Royce's house. He was driving a brand new Mercedes G-Wagon and dressed like a fancy cowboy. Royce came out of his house when he saw him and pointed for him to get back in his rig. They had a quiet, big gestured argument for a few minutes, and then the guy left."

"When was this?"

"Friday afternoon, around three. I was outside getting my car packed to leave when it happened."

"What makes you think that the man was the one to meet with Royce?"

Meadow took a bite of mozzarella stick and chewed, obviously choosing her words carefully. "I could overhear bits and pieces of their conversation. Mostly it was Royce saying he shouldn't be here, and then at the end Royce said he would see him later and not to come to his house again. I had the impression Royce didn't want the two of them to be seen together. So if he was going to meet someone up at the hot springs that night, I bet it was that guy."

Sadie considered that as she took a drink of beer. "What else can you tell me about him?"

"City slicker. Wearing cowboy boots in the snow, pressed blue jeans, ten gallon hat."

That description could be any Jackson Hole tourist or new-to-town developer, but something about it tickled Sadie's brain. The developer who'd wanted to meet with Paige at brunch. What had his name been? Hadn't Paige said that he owned land near Hoback Junction?

"Did you tell the detective about that?"

"Of course," Meadow said, wiping her hands on a napkin. "He didn't seem that interested, though."

"Did you ever have any trouble with Royce?"

Meadow pulled a face. "All the time. He was supposed to be the guy that fixed things around the compound, but every time I needed anything, it was like pulling teeth. He was always jumping in to help people in the permanent housing, but he took weeks to fix my washing machine. Do you know how annoying it is to haul laundry around in the snow?"

"DeeDee said she saw you arguing with him last week."

Meadow snorted. "I'm sure she did. Anything to get the suspicion off her. You know she advocated for tearing down the old houses and making everything permanent trailer pads? She hates that her neighbors turn over all the time because of the three-year limit. She's all about 'preserving the neighborhood character' and if you ask me, she means keeping out anyone who can't afford to buy a mobile home. And have you seen the prices on those lately?"

Sadie had, in fact, seen the prices on them lately. Long the cheapest house per square foot, mobile home prices had shot up due to supply chain issues. "I didn't know that. I heard her say something about preserving neighborhood character and wondered what that meant to her, though."

"Royce was on her about her pyramid scheme–excuse me–her home-based business, too. He'd found some policy that stated it wasn't allowed, or required Ranger approval, or something like that, and was threatening her over it. Just like he did to Jerry."

So Darnell's suspicion had been true. Interesting. "Threatening her how? Her and Jerry both are in permanent housing."

"I'm not sure. I saw her crying about it in one of her Facebook lives, though. You should check and see if it's still up." Meadow stood up. "Thanks for the beer. And for poking around in this. I want nothing to do with it, like I said, and I also don't want to be living with a murderer. I'm headed out to stay with my boyfriend and remote work for the next week or so. Get this figured out so I can come home, yeah?"

Sadie gave her a weak smile. "I'll try. Thanks."

Meadow left. As she did, Sadie realized she'd never told her what she'd argued with Royce about a week ago that DeeDee had overheard. But, if she was out of town the night he was murdered, it probably didn't matter. Being hours away was a pretty good alibi.

* * *

Sadie stayed at the brewpub long enough the lights dimmed, the music got louder, and the crush in the bar got tighter as more young people packed in to yell in each other's ears about their ski slope triumphs, graduate theses, and favorite TikToks. At least, that's what Sadie thought young people yelled to each other about these days. She finished the second beer she'd been nursing and signed the slip Nash put in front of her.

"I'm headed out, too," he said, tipping his head towards her so she could hear him, a lock of red hair falling over his forehead as he did. "I'll walk you home."

"You don't have to do that," Sadie protested. She stood and pulled her coat and hat on. Nash was already coming around the bar, though, pulling on his own winter gear. Sadie could tell from the look on his face that he wouldn't be deterred, so she shrugged and let him lead her through the crush of bodies and out the door into the cold winter air.

The crowd around the bonfire hadn't thinned and had grown wilder as the evening wore on. Nash eyed them as they walked by, but didn't stop. They turned out onto the sidewalk to make their way to Sadie's, companionable silence between them as they strolled past the bars and restaurants and then into the quiet blocks.

Finally, Nash spoke. "Seen Penny lately?"

"Just the other night, actually. Why?" Sadie peeked up at Nash and saw his cheekbones were tinged red.

He cleared his throat. "Just haven't seen her in a bit, is all."

"Hmm."

"She uh...dating Gregg Knott?"

"I think it's almost official, yes."

Nash frowned, and Sadie hid a smile. Nash had been pining after Penny for years, but had never made a move.

"He doesn't seem her type," he said finally, his voice a low grumble.

They approached Sadie's house. There were a few more cars than normal parked outside, and the lights were on in the basement windows. Sadie could hear music pumping. KitKat was having a get together. They came to a stop on the sidewalk.

Sadie turned to Nash. "I can't tell you anything about their relationship. It wouldn't be fair. But I can tell you that if you have feelings for her, you should tell her already."

Nash averted his eyes, but finally nodded. "Right."

"Right."

"Now, I'm going inside and going to bed. Thanks for walking me home. You're a good friend." They hugged, and Sadie turned towards her house while Nash turned towards his condo a few blocks away. Her phone buzzed in her pocket and she plucked it out. A text from Kendall sent to a large group:

KAMARI JUST GOT CAST IN A NEW TGR FILM COME CELEBRATE WITH US

Sadie's breath caught, and she gave a squeal. That was huge! Getting cast to ski in a film by the internationally known local production company, Teton Gravity Research, would be a major boon for her career.

She turned to call after Nash, but he was already headed back towards her, phone in hand and a grin on his face. He held his phone up to her. "I just got invited to a party at your house!"

Sadie laughed. "Me too."

He joined her, and Sadie checked her watch as they approached the basement apartment entrance. It was 10:30 p.m., and she had to open the bakery the next day. And she'd already had two beers. But what was another drink to toast her friend?

# Chapter Fifteen

Sadie and Nash were the last of the friend group to arrive. The main living area was packed with people, and the bedroom doors were open, more people spilling out of them. A pile of snow boots crowded the entrance, and a rainbow pile of puffy coats covered a nearby chair. What she had presumed was a stereo system pumping out music was actually a Princess-Leia-bunned DJ setup on the kitchen table bopping enthusiastically as she spun records. A projector showed a classic Warren Miller ski film against one wall. An enthusiastic group was dancing in the kitchen, the table shoved over to the side and covered with liquor bottles and a punch bowl filled with murky liquid. The lights were dim, and twinkle lights were criss-crossed on the ceiling, giving a starry night effect. The apartment stunk of fireball whiskey, patchouli oil, and wet GORE-TEX jackets.

And even over all that noise, Sadie could still hear the Moose's Bakery crew.

Her head swiveled at the sound of them and she laughed as she took them in, a tight-knit group in the corner. Kamari was grinning wider than Sadie had ever seen her. She was surrounded by her friends and coworkers, including Max, Sage, Rachael, and even Jorge, her weekday manager, a retired high school football coach. Kendall was standing next to her, chest puffed out like a proud parent, her arms flapping as she told a story. She caught sight of Sadie and Nash, pointed and nudged everyone, and they all yelled, "Moose!" loud enough the DJ stopped the music. Sadie's face burned as everyone turned to look at her. She gave a self-conscious wave at the crowd, then hustled over to the group, Nash right behind her.

She bundled Kamari up in her arms first.

"I'm so proud of you!" Sadie said, yelling over the music that had restarted louder than before.

"Thanks, Sadie," Kamari said. "This means I won't be at the bakery as much..."

Sadie shrugged. "We'll miss you, but I cannot wait to watch you shredding on the big screen!"

Kamari danced in place and threw her arms in the air. "It's going to be so fucking awesome!"

Everyone in the circle joined her in her joy, jumping up and down. Someone brought over a tray of shots, and for the next hour, Sadie's world was a blur of cinnamon whiskey, eighties hair rock the DJ spun together with modern TikTok hits, and bodies crashing together as they danced in joy.

Max did the robot, complete with beeping and booping sounds.

Jorge pulled Kamari into a complicated two-step.

Kendall showed off the latest TikTok dance.

Nash bobbed back and forth.

Rachael dropped it like it was hot, then dropped it again.

Sage drifted, her arms wide, dancing as always to a beat no one else could hear.

Sadie did her signature three moves—foot to foot, arms up, shimmy—then repeat.

In between songs, they gulped drinks, chatted over each other, and listened to Kamari tell the story over and over again about how she'd been cast in the film.

Eventually exhausted, Sadie slipped into a recently vacated couch seat, laughing. The party continued around her, louder and more boisterous than before. She had a good view from her position, and she let herself people watch, her eyes drifting over the dancing bodies. With a start, she zeroed in on three people she'd been looking for all day—the roommates that lived in number six. Her brain was fuzzy with booze and a need for sleep, but she shook her head to clear it. She got up, grabbed a cold bottle of water out of a cooler, and turned to where the three stood by the front door, watching the crowd.

* * *

They were two girls and one guy, and as Sadie squeezed through the crowd toward them, the taller blonde girl noticed her and elbowed her companions, a brunette girl with a nose piercing and a sandy-haired boy with glasses. When she arrived in front of them, they all watched her cooly.

Sadie took a swig of her water. "Hi," she said, smiling. "I'm Sadie Moose. I've been meaning to introduce myself to you, but haven't gotten a chance."

They stared at her. Sadie took another drink.

"How do you know Kamari?"

The blonde looked at the other girl, and they both looked at the boy. Finally, the brunette spoke up.

"Everyone knows Kamari. But we know her from the resort." She paused, her green eyes flicking around the room, then landing on Sadie again. "I'm Megan, by the way. This is Sydney and Travis." Sydney and Travis both raised their hands in half waves.

"It's nice to meet all of you."

They were silent for a few minutes, then Travis spoke up.

"We didn't kill Royce, if that's what you're wondering."

Sadie shrugged. "Okay. I heard you three are losing your housing in the spring. I'm sorry about that. I don't get why the Forest only lets you have three years. It's not like there's anywhere else to go."

Sydney made an I-know-right face but continued to not speak. Megan's face had pulled into a scowl. "It's the worst. We're so mad about it. We asked for a year's extension because we've heard of people getting them before, but Royce wouldn't go to bat for us with the Ranger and they denied it."

"He said his preference was to have 'families' in housing. Like he gets to define what a family is, or his preference should matter. He's not in charge." Travis looked upset, and Sydney put her hand over his. Sadie readjusted the dynamic in her head. Were Travis and Sydney were together? Then Megan put her hand in Travis's other one, and laid her head on his shoulder. Or maybe they were all three together. Sadie mentally shrugged. Whatever worked for them.

"That's infuriating, I'm so sorry. I wonder if the Ranger would hear your appeal now, without him in the way?"

Megan sighed. "We'd need someone else to go to support us. Actually." Megan straightened, lifting her head off of Travis's shoulder. "Would Jake?"

"Oh, I'm not sure. You could definitely ask him."

"Could you ask him for us?" Travis looked at her pleadingly.

"Oh. I can bring it up? But y'all are his neighbors."

"We have social anxiety," Megan explained. "We already had to talk to you. If you ask him, we don't have to be anxious about talking to him."

Sadie suppressed a sigh. "Okay. I'll ask him. Where were you guys the night Royce was murdered, though?"

"Sydney was working a shift at the Cowboy Bar. Travis and I were there, keeping her company. None of us got home until after the bars closed at two."

Sadie tried to picture the silent, deadpan Sydney working the crowd at the popular tourist attraction, the Million Dollar Cowboy Bar, where the barstools were saddles and a country band played every night, and failed. Maybe she saved all her energy for those nights.

"Do you know who might've wanted to kill Royce?"

"Who didn't, really?" Megan asked philosophically, her gaze floating over the crowd. Kendall looked to be arranging a game of limbo. Was it strip limbo? Why was the crowd suddenly much less dressed than they'd been moments ago?

"We try not to get involved in neighborhood drama," Travis said. "But of anyone I've seen arguing with Royce in the last few months, the worst was when him and Cole got into it a few weeks ago. Cole is a big guy, and I thought he was going to throttle Royce."

Sadie didn't like the sound of that.

"Do you know why they were arguing?"

"I couldn't hear the details. I just saw it. They didn't see me. They were over by the big log pile and I was out looking for one of our dogs. Cole had Royce backed up against the logs, and he wasn't yelling, but the look on his face was murderous." Travis gave a small shake of his shoulders. "There's a reason we didn't ask him to support our petition."

Sydney broke away then, joining the growing line to try the limbo. The DJ had cranked the music, and Kendall was, of course, filming on her phone.

"I want to go limbo, too," Megan looked at Sadie apologetically. "We don't know anything else. Hit us up when Jake gives an answer, okay?" She pulled Travis's hand, and they left Sadie standing there.

Sadie yawned hugely. She looked at her watch and frowned. She had to be up in a few hours to open the bakery. Time to be a grown up. She made her way to the door, looking around for Nash. He was cozied up in the corner talking to a dark-haired woman, and Sadie smiled. That was good. He needed to move on if he would never confess his feelings to Penny. Sadie yawned again. She had enough to think about tonight. She'd leave the kids—and Nash—to their partying, go upstairs, make herself a cup of tea, take two Advil, turn on her white noise as loud as possible, and go to bed. In the morning, she had a bakery to open, and a murderer to find.

# Chapter Sixteen

Sadie wasn't sure what time the party underneath her wrapped up the night before, but Kendall still showed up at the bakery bright eyed at 5:15 a.m. to pick up the pastries for the coffee kiosk. She looked better than Sadie felt.

"Hey Boss," she yawned as she came in through the back, pep in her step despite the yawning. "Great news about Kamari, yeah?"

Sadie was elbows deep in rolling out scones, her head pounding. "The best news. I'm glad you threw her a party."

"It was pretty good. Strip limbo got a little wild, but naked Twister is always a hit after."

Sadie narrowed her eyes at Kendall, who was innocently stacking bakery boxes. She could be pulling Sadie's old millennial chain, or she could be serious. Gen Z was inscrutable, as far as Sadie was concerned. She settled on a noncommittal "hmmm" and continued rolling out her cheddar and chive scones, slightly hungover and refusing to take the bait.

"Kamari will come by when the champagne wears off to talk about her schedule." Kendall loaded up boxes in her arms and headed for the door.

"Whatever she needs," Sadie said, her mind ticking through the shuffling that would need to be done if Kamari took a leave of absence. With the possibility of Kendall moving into a more managerial role—which they still needed to talk about—and Kamari hitting the big time in her true passion, it was probably time for Sadie to recruit more baristas. She shuddered to think of putting another ad in the Jackson Hole Journal. The last time she'd picked up the paper, there'd been thirteen pages of help wanted ads. Contrast that with the single column of rentals combined with the lack of real estate listings for under one million, and hiring in Jackson was a bit of an ordeal. And with KitKat living in her basement, she didn't have any other housing to offer. Her mind drifted to the house the O'Donnells were currently living in.

When Merritt had given her the deed to that house, a project to convert the entire block, including Sadie's childhood home, into luxury condominiums had been on the table, with thirty percent of the homeowners on the block on board to sell. The deal had since fallen through, both because the person pushing it had been found dead in the alley behind Sadie's house, and because current housing rules enacted by the town council wouldn't allow it. Sadie didn't want to lose her home, but it was tempting, when she thought about it, to use the two houses she now controlled on the block to leverage a workforce housing complex. It would be the right thing to do. But could Sadie sacrifice her home to do it?

The door opened again and Kendall came in for her last stack of boxes.

"Snowing out there again," she commented, hefting the last stack. "Wish me luck on the drive and with my trainees today." Travis was back today, and Holly was working her first shift.

"Luck," Sadie said, finishing up cutting the scones and transferring them to baking sheets. Kendall stepped back out, and the bakery was quiet again except for the podcast Sadie had playing over the kitchen speakers. A timer beeped, and Sadie turned to deal with it. She put the larger community housing issue out of her head, along with her hiring needs. For this morning, at least, she could be just a baker, albeit a slightly hungover one, and lose herself in the process.

Sadie's phone ringing brought her out of her baking trance. She frowned at the wall clock. It was a little after six o'clock. Who would call her at this hour? Was it Max, due in at seven, calling out sick?

She grabbed a towel and rubbed the flour off her hands, stepping away from the pastry dough she was laminating to pick her phone up off the counter. It was Kendall. Frowning, Sadie picked up.

"Kendall, what's up?"

There was a pause. "It's not good, Boss," Kendall cautioned.

Sadie's stomach dropped.

"Are you okay?" Her voice was tinged with panic.

"I'm okay. Everyone's okay. But our beautiful kiosk is...not."

* * *

Kendall hadn't overstated it. When Sadie pulled up forty-five minutes later, having hastily pulled the bakes out of the ovens and locked up, knowing Max could pick up where she left off when they got in, her heart sank even further. The flashing police lights cast the scene in stark relief. The kiosk's windows, smashed open. The back door, kicked in. Sadie couldn't see the inside, but Kendall had told her it was trashed, and poor Francesca had taken damage. It felt like a message to Sadie, a personal affront to her. As she got out of her car and walked around the side of the kiosk, she realized it was more than just a veiled attack on her. It was blatant.

Written in powder blue spray paint were the words NOSY BITCH.

Sadie stood, staring, her breaths coming quickly. This wasn't random vandalism, or an attempted robbery. This was a warning to her. A threat. Stop asking questions, or else.

"...Moose?" A voice finally broke through the roaring in her ears. She looked around and saw Kendall standing close, a concerned look on her face.

"Oh, Kendall," Sadie said, her eyes tearing up. "I'm so glad you're safe."

"They were long gone by the time I got here, boss," Kendall assured her, laying a hand on her arm. "I sent Travis and Holly home."

Right. Another thing to worry about. She'd just hired three new employees, and they'd be out of work until they could get this cleaned up. Who knew how long the fixes to Francesca would take. That was the problem with fancy Italian espresso machines—mechanics weren't close by. "Right," Sadie said, finally. She took a deep breath, and then another, and then squared her shoulders. "Have you talked to the police?"

"It's the county sheriff, and yeah. They want to talk to you, too. They're taking pictures right now."

"Oh! The security cameras!"

Kendall shrugged. "I checked. They took them out before they showed themselves. This was definitely a planned out job. The cameras went dark around three, one after another."

Sadie peered at the awnings of the kiosk, where the cameras overlooked the windows and back door. Someone could approach from the front, she saw now, and use some sort of long-handled device, or...a slingshot? God. Sure. Maybe a slingshot, and disable the cameras one by one, working around the building without being seen. Even at the intersection of a major highway, in the parking lot of a market, with homes scattered around the junction, it would be easy to do it without being seen. Three in the morning wasn't a busy time in Hoback Junction, Wyoming. Sadie thought about Jake. Had he been out grooming last night? He would have called her if he'd driven by the kiosk and saw it in this state, though.

"Damn," Sadie said. "I should've installed them in a different array, I guess. Next time."

"At least there wasn't cash for them to grab. Actually, as far as I can see, nothing is missing. Just destroyed."

Sadie groaned. "I'll call our insurance company and put in a service request with the repair guy as soon as I'm done with the sheriff, then."

"I took pictures. Can I call someone to board up the windows?"

"You're a saint, and yes." Sadie saw a woman in a sheriff's deputy uniform round the corner of the kiosk, and Sadie stood up a little straighter at the stern look on the woman's face. Kendall stepped away to make a call.

"Ms. Moose?" The woman had a gruff voice. She was the same height as Sadie, which is to say she was short, and stout, with hawkish features. Sadie guessed she was in her late forties.

"Yes, ma'am," Sadie said automatically.

"I'm sorry for the damage that occurred here," the deputy said, her voice softening a hair. "I'm Deputy Smith. We've taken photos and I have a guy coming out to dust for fingerprints. I'm not sure it will help, considering it was subzero last night at three o'clock when the break in probably occurred, but better safe than sorry. We'll need you and anyone else that works here to report down to the station for fingerprinting so we can rule them out."

"Oh, yes." Sadie was a little surprised they were taking this so seriously. "It's just me, Kendall, who you met, and Travis, so far. I'll make sure they know."

"We reviewed the security cameras through Ms. Craig's phone, and unfortunately, we didn't get any leads. We'll ask around about other cameras, but for now..." her voice trailed off as she turned to face the kiosk, so she and Sadie were standing shoulder to shoulder. She gestured at the message on the wood siding. "Know anyone that's trying to send you a message?"

Sadie gulped. "Well...my boyfriend and I were the one to find Royce Hensley's body last Friday."

Deputy Smith stiffened, and she looked at Sadie again.

"Is that right?"

"Yes. Maybe this is related to that."

The deputy narrowed her eyes at her. "So you live down in Poplar with your boyfriend?"

"No, I live in Jackson. My boyfriend lives in Poplar, though."

The deputy looked off into the distance. "I need to make a phone call."

"Can I call our insurer?" Sadie said as she went to leave.

"Yes. But stay here." Sadie winced. She'd done a great job of avoiding the penetrating electric blue gaze of Detective Will Nolan so far, and she'd like to keep it that way. Didn't sound like she had much of a choice, though. With a sigh, she looked at her phone, pulling off a glove so her fingers could swipe it open and scroll through her contacts until she found the number for her local insurance agent. It wasn't quite eight o'clock, but Sandeep Singh had been the Moose's insurance agent since the nineties. He'd be apoplectic if she didn't call him right away.

Sadie was hanging up with Sandeep when she felt a warm hand on her shoulder. She turned to see Jake's concerned face under a stocking cap, his eyes sleepy, dark rings underneath, and her face crumpled. He pulled her into him, wrapping his muscular arms around her.

Sadie's shoulders shook as she let herself cry into his

embrace. Jake stroked her back and whispered nonsense comforting words against the knit of her hat. The last thing Sadie wanted was for anyone to see her this way. Thinking of the person who had done this seeing her this way made her want to pull herself out of Jake's arms, dry her eyes, and set her shoulders. She didn't want to appear broken. She didn't want to appear affected by someone's act of intimidation. But it didn't work that way. You couldn't choose when to have a breakdown. Sometimes, you just had to let the emotion flow. And so she did. She let herself feel fear. She let herself feel anger. She let herself feel dumb. Why had she poked around in this business, anyway? She wasn't some amateur detective. She was a bakery owner who liked puzzles and had an aptitude for stumbling onto dead bodies. If she'd kept her nose out of it, this wouldn't have happened. That must be what everyone else was thinking, too. And that's when Sadie felt the familiar feeling of embarrassment. How silly everyone must think she was.

Her tears finally dried up. She took some steady breaths and finally pulled away from Jake. She looked up at him, and his face was pinched with concern.

"I'm so sorry this happened," he said finally.

Sadie sniffled. "It's my fault."

Jake blinked at her, then frowned. "How's that?"

"If I hadn't poked around in Royce's death, this wouldn't have happened. They're right. I'm a nosy bitch."

Jake jerked his head back as if someone had slapped him. "Stop that."

Sadie pulled herself out of his arms. "You were thinking the same thing."

His jaw tightened as his arms dropped to his sides. "Don't presume to know what I was thinking."

"I'm sure everyone's thinking it," Sadie said, her voice a little wild. "Silly Sadie Moose, sticking her nose where it doesn't belong and paying for it."

Jake held his hands up in front of him in a calming gesture. It made Sadie irate. She wasn't a horse to be motioned to "woah."

"I hear what you're saying," he said finally, in a calm voice. "And I think you're letting yourself spiral a little here. This is a traumatic thing that happened."

She was spiraling. He was right. The edges of her vision were blackening. Her fingers were tingling, and it wasn't just from the cold.

*Oh, right. I have anxiety.* Sometimes Sadie forgot, from one dose of medication to the next. And sometimes she walked around feeling like the earth might swallow her any moment, like every step was closer to calamity. Sometimes her brain told her lies, that everyone hated her, that everyone thought she was dumb, that everyone would leave her, eventually. But most of the time, the medication helped. As did breathing exercises, which Sadie immediately started doing. Suddenly, Kendall was there, and her hand was grasping Sadie's, breathing with her.

"Let's get you sat down," Jake said after a moment. "Somewhere warm."

They bundled Sadie into Jake's truck, putting a blanket over her shoulders and turning the heat up. Jake had brought a thermos of hot water, and he fixed her a cup of tea. He pulled off her gloves and put the warm cup into them, looking into her eyes.

"I'm sorry I freaked on you there," Sadie said quietly, averting her eyes. Jake hadn't seen her have a panic attack before.

"It's a freaky situation, Moose," he said gently, leaning in to press a kiss to her forehead. "The only thing I was thinking when Kendall called was one, how will I keep you safe. And two, I will find the person who did this and make them pay."

Sadie's heart squeezed. She was a lucky woman to have Jake. To have Kendall. To have her whole circle of friends and employees and customers. They loved her like she loved them. They watched out for her like she did for them. And that meant sometimes she asked questions, so they wouldn't get into trouble. The only person who was responsible for her kiosk being destroyed was the person who had done it. And Sadie, being a nosy bitch, was going to find out who it was.

# Chapter Seventeen

Sadie watched Jake and Kendall board up her windows once they were given the go ahead by the deputy. She felt bad, sitting in the warm truck drinking tea while they worked, but they'd insisted she should rest. They'd be able to clean out the kiosk once the detective arrived and had a look around, and Sadie needed to help with that.

Speaking of the detective.

An unmarked black SUV pulled up behind the deputy's vehicle and he stepped out. He was white and tall with a lean build. Today he wore a black micro-puff coat and black slacks, with a black watch cap pulled down over his ears. Sadie hadn't spoken to him in a few weeks, since he'd come into the bakery last for a shot in the dark and a scone, his regular order. Sadie wasn't quite sure what to think of him, every time they talked. During the last investigation she'd been entangled in, he'd seen her first as the chief suspect, then as a pest, and then as a victim he'd failed to protect from another crime. Less than a week later, Sadie had stumbled upon the actual killer, so he'd been caught with egg on his face as he had the wrong person locked up. Ever since then, he'd been overly conciliatory to her, and it made her feel off balance. Like she couldn't tell if he was telling the truth. She'd also seen him in a silly Halloween costume to appease his son that lived with him summers and some holidays, and seeing him as a fun dad had put her off kilter a bit. It was easier to imagine him as RoboCop instead of a man with thoughts, feelings, and a personal life.

She watched as he walked around the kiosk, peering up at the cameras, examining the words, getting close to the paint, and then going inside for a few minutes before coming back out. He spoke briefly to Kendall and Jake as they lifted a sheet of plywood to cover the window facing the parking lot, and she saw them wave him towards her.

Apparently, it was her turn.

When he approached Jake's truck, Sadie waved awkwardly. He lifted a hand to wave as well, then gestured at the driver's side door. Sadie pushed the unlock button, and after a second of hesitation, he climbed inside. The space felt very small suddenly, and he brought the scent of outside—crisp wind, coffee, minty aftershave, and exhaust—with him. They were silent for a moment.

"I'm sorry about this trouble," he said finally, looking right at her.

"Thanks," Sadie said. She tried to hold his gaze, but glanced away. He was an intense guy, and she was feeling a little fragile. She wasn't sure she wanted his piercing blue eyes to see through her right now.

"I looked around. They used the same blue paint to cover your cameras. Must've had quite the range on the spray can."

"Huh."

"Know anyone that's sprayed anything powder blue lately?"

Sadie thought about it. "I don't. Kind of odd choice."

"Yep. Know anyone that has a grudge against you at the moment?"

Sadie bristled a bit at his qualification, like she had people lining up with grudges against her. She couldn't think of more than...five people that were currently angry with her, and all of them were because of her outspoken support for affordable housing.

"I can't think of anyone with a grudge *at the moment*," she said, her voice steely.

Detective Nolan looked out the front window, where Jake was holding the plywood as Kendall used a cordless drill to affix it.

"Someone doesn't like that you're asking questions about Royce Hensley's death," he said finally, flatly. "It's a police matter, and I can assure you that I'm investigating it thoroughly. You can stop. It would be best for your safety."

Sadie was silent for a moment. Jake and Kendall were done with that window and were moving on to the next. Another car, one of many, pulled up, slowing before they realized they weren't getting coffee today and moving on. Another customer, lost. More money, out the door. Was Sadie's investigation going to cost her business? She'd learned last time it could cost her life.

"All I've done is ask some questions," she said finally. "I haven't really found anything out."

"Someone must think you have." He pulled off his cap and ran his hand over his short cropped dark hair.

That was true. She must have struck a chord with someone to earn this kind of response.

"Did you get the test results on Amos Garner back yet?"

Detective Nolan gave a short bark of laughter. "You don't know when to stop, do you?"

"Just wondering. He'll tell me if you don't, so you might as well tell me."

"Is that who you're doing it for? Amos?"

"His Gran is one of my best customers. And he seems like a nice kid trying to make better decisions."

"I can't tell you what we found, but I can tell you he wasn't drunk."

"So he's not a suspect anymore, then?"

"Next question."

At least he was consenting to being questioned.

"Find anything good at Jerry's house?"

"I can't answer that."

Sadie sighed.

Detective Nolan sighed.

"I can promise you I will investigate this vandalism with the same vigor I'm investigating the murder."

"Isn't it a sheriff's case?"

"I've deemed it related, so I and my officers will investigate it."

"Well, thanks, then."

The detective turned toward her then, giving her a hard look. "Please try to stay out of this case. I don't want you to get hurt."

It struck Sadie as a very personal statement. *He* didn't want her to get hurt. Him, Will Nolan? Or him, detective on the Jackson Hole Police Department, responsible for public safety, which would include her? Before she could wrap her head around that, her door was opening, and Jake was standing there.

"All good in here?" He asked. His voice was bright, maybe overly so.

"All good," Detective Nolan said. "Remember what I said, Sadie." He got out of the car, pulling his stocking cap back on and walking briskly over to the sheriff's deputy.

Sadie watched him, then turned to Jake. He raised his eyebrows at her. "He just wants me to stop asking questions."

Jake shrugged. "Of course he does. He knows you'll solve the case right out from underneath him."

Sadie laughed. "So you're not going to tell me to stop?"

"I know better than to tell you anything, Moose. I'm just going to stay close to you to help keep you safe." He leaned in and brushed a kiss across her lips. Sadie sighed and leaned in. Jake smelled like fresh cut wood, wood smoke, and freshly greased boots, a distinctive wildland firefighter smell that always made Sadie smile. She did so now, smiling against his lips before pulling away.

"We're all done here," he said, his voice low. "Come home with me?"

"I need to help clean up," she protested.

"Kendall says she's got it. Travis is coming back to help her. I brought a padlock, and we rigged the door for now, until you can get it replaced."

"I have so many calls to make," she said. "I should do it from my office."

"My house is cozy, has internet and cell service, and you'll be close to me," he bargained. "Plus, I have a bed, for when you inevitably need a nap later. You seem a little hungover still."

That tipped the scales in his favor. "Fine. Let me go check in with Kendall, and then I'll be back."

* * *

By mid-morning, Sadie had a contractor lined up to come fix the door and a window company coming to replace the glass. The espresso machine mechanic was booked out a week, but Sadie had cajoled him into coming up from his base in central Idaho with the promise of letting him also do regular service on the machine in her bakery, and the added work had made him consent to come in two days. It was Wednesday, and it looked like if all went well, they might open again on Saturday.

She still needed to work on replacing the security cameras and ordering new supplies to replace what had been ruined—or stolen, but she had a good start on her to do list. They'd gone through things more thoroughly before Sadie had left the kiosk and realized there was one thing completely missing...the bag of cinnamon moose they distributed with their drinks. So the culprit had a sweet tooth, apparently? How bizarre. Sandeep was already filing her claim, so with luck she'd see reimbursement funds to cover the costs soon. Kendall and Travis were going into town to fingerprinted. Sadie planned to go the next day.

She'd called to check in with Max, who'd bolted over to the bakery early after she'd called them in a panic this morning. They reported everything was going well, and she didn't need to come in for the day. Which was good, because Sadie didn't want to leave the cozy cabin. The wood stove was roaring, Jake was taking a nap—his regular sleep schedule having been interrupted by her emergency this morning—the doors were locked, a light snow was falling outside, and she had a pot of coffee and a box of baked goods all to herself.

Suddenly remembering her conversation with Meadow last night, Sadie picked up her phone and sent a text to Paige.

```
What was the name of that developer that
talked to us at brunch? Did you ever meet
with him?
```

Sadie munched on a croissant as she scrolled through the bakery's social media feed and waited for Paige's response. She'd taken a box of leftover baked goods with her when she'd left, telling Kendall and Travis to take what they wanted and donate the rest in town. She posted an update about the kiosk being closed, asking her followers to contact the police department if they had any info that could help them find the culprit. Calling people to action always made her social media posts get more traction. She didn't expect anyone would have anything to share, though.

Her phone vibrated, and Sadie checked the response she'd gotten from Paige.

`Preston Chandler, ugh. And my meeting with him is scheduled for tomorrow. Why?`

Sadie sent a quick "no reason" text back to Paige, promising to call her later. She had a name now, which meant she could look him up.

Aimlessly, she scrolled through her social media. Her mind was whirling with information. Suspects. Who had an alibi. What had actually happened that night. She paused as a live video popped up on her feed. It was her friend Amy from college, doing a product tutorial for the multi-level marketing company she represented. She remembered, suddenly, what Meadow had told her about DeeDee's makeup business. She typed DeeDee's name into the search bar, and her profile popped up at the top. Sadie clicked on it.

Her profile photo showed her in complicated makeup, her hair teased, with a big grin on her face. She was wearing a hot pink lanyard, and when Sadie clicked the photo, she could make out enough of the name tag to read that the picture had been taken at the makeup company's conference in Nashville, Tennessee. She was deep into it then, if she'd flown all the way to Nashville to attend.

Sadie clicked back into her feed, scrolling through pictures of kids and lots of links to the makeup she was selling. Finally, she came to a live video, and she clicked on it. It had been posted two weeks ago. In it, DeeDee sat in front of the camera, her well-lit face twisted in sadness.

"I have sad news," she began. "Oh hey, hun!" She interrupted herself, her voice going from somber to stoked whiplash fast. She said hello to a few more people, then settled back into her somber tone. "I've been told I can't run my business here as I have been." Tears filled her eyes. "I'm being persecuted for running a successful women-led business out of my home." The tears started streaming from her eyes, and DeeDee used a tissue to blot at them. Sadie narrowed her eyes. Her heavily-applied mascara and eyeliner weren't running. That was some seriously heavy duty waterproof makeup. DeeDee started replying to the outpouring of comments that were coming in on her video. Yes, it was an outrage. Yes, she was fighting it. Yes, it was really unfair. Sadie kept watching, expecting to see DeeDee name the culprit that was working against her, but it didn't come. Eventually, DeeDee transitioned the video into sales, and ended it with a call to action for her supporters to send her an email supporting her and her business she could take with her when she went to discuss it with the Ranger.

So DeeDee had lied to her when she'd told her she hadn't recently had an argument with Royce. Royce had turned in her home-based business to the Ranger as well. Sadie wondered if DeeDee had attended that meeting yet, and what the outcome had been if she had.

Sadie searched for Royce Hensley, but he wasn't on social media as far as she could find. She opened her Instagram, switching from her frequently used bakery account to her much-less-used personal account, and was surprised to see a few notifications. She clicked through them. Bots following her—she blocked them. A message from a wellness coach with an "opportunity". Gross. Blocked. And one in her spam folder that caught her eye. The sender was named JH007, and the profile pic was of a lion. Sadie stared at the message for a moment, then guiltily peered down the hallway to where she could hear Jake lightly snoring, making sure he was still asleep before she opened the message.

She held her breath as she clicked it.

It was short.

You can stop looking for me on social media. Will you be my only follower?

Sadie smothered a short laugh and realized she was grinning at her laptop. With shaky hands, she clicked on JH007's profile —who could only be Merritt West, long absent from social media and her life, except from their brief but intense encounter last fall, and clicked request to follow. He had no followers, and followed only her. He was going to have to approve her request. Sadie sat there for a moment, drumming her fingers on the table as if he would do it while she waited. He didn't of course, and finally Sadie closed Instagram and shut the lid of her laptop.

She felt jittery and off balance. Too much coffee, too much stress, and too much excitement at a possible link to Merritt. She told herself, again, that she needed to get over him. He wasn't leaving his job in Washington D.C. and she wasn't leaving Jackson. It wasn't meant to be between them.

Jake hit a particularly high note snoring, and she shook herself. She had Jake. Maybe not forever, but they were exploring where it would go. He was a nice man. A sweet, happy, caring man. One that knew he couldn't control her, but still wanted to keep her safe. And he was handsome and held her in his arms with strength and comfort. Sadie felt a thrill go through her, and she realized they were alone, with no obligations. And there was a bed. She needed to focus on the man who was here, with her, and not on the man that wouldn't be around again.

# Chapter Eighteen

Sadie slipped into bed beside Jake and he turned toward her, eyes closed, to snuggle against her. She burrowed in, putting one hand on his cheek, running it over his soft, crinkly beard, and turning his lips down to meet hers.

"Mmmm..." he murmured, his lips sleepily returning her kiss. His arms closed around her, and his eyes popped open. "Are you...ooh, you are," he said with surprise, then satisfaction, as he realized she'd climbed into bed next to him naked.

His hand smoothed over her back, across the swell of her belly and hip, to her thigh, to the curve of her ass. He groaned. "You're so soft."

Sadie wriggled closer to him.

He rolled her onto her back, coming over her, one leg over her hips. He kissed his way down her neck. "You always smell so good. Like cinnamon and sugar and coffee."

Sadie giggled. "I smell like a baked good?"

"And you taste as good as one, too."

"You always smell like freshly cut trees."

"I bet I taste better than one, though."

Sadie nipped at his neck. "You do."

Jake's head moved lower, burrowing between her breasts. He caught one nipple between his fingers and Sadie's breath caught. He tugged, and warmth pooled between her thighs. He moved his mouth over the stiff peak and suckled, and she groaned.

Jake moved down her body, drawing big open-mouthed kisses over her curves, licking and nipping until he was positioned between her thighs. Sadie felt the tickle of his beard on her sensitive skin, the pressure of his hands as he pushed her legs apart, making room to drop kisses, run his tongue across the sensitive crease where her leg met thigh. She felt his hot breath, and she wriggled in anticipation of feeling his mouth at her center, but he held her thighs firm.

When he finally lowered his mouth to her, she couldn't contain her moan of pleasure. With powerful fingers, an agile tongue, and focus of attention, she came apart under him quickly, a bright hot flash of pleasure rolling into a languid unfurling of tension from her limbs. When he kissed himself back up her body, she clutched him.

"Sugar and spice," he said, nuzzling her neck. "I remembered from before. I missed the taste of you."

Sadie's hand stole down his body, under the athletic boxer briefs he wore to palm his length. "I missed you, too," she murmured.

Jake groaned as she wrapped her hand around him, giving him a long, languid stroke.

"Condoms?" She asked.

"In the drawer on your side," he said, gasping, "if you want to. We don't have to."

Sadie met his eyes. "I want to. I want you."

They kissed, and then Jake dug around in the bedside table for a condom. He sheathed his length, then lowered himself between Sadie's legs.

When they were finally joined, a deep peace overtook Sadie. There was pleasure building, which they crested together, their voices mingling into moans as they both plateaued, but the peace within her was a balm for her soul. Jake was the right man for her for where she was now. He could be the right man for her forever, maybe. As they lay together in the afterglow, her heartbeat slowly calming, the weight of Jake pressed into her side, she let her eyes close. Murder, and motives, and means, were far from her mind.

* * *

It was late afternoon when Sadie and Jake were awoken from their post-coital snooze by a brisk knock on the door. Jake groaned and threw an arm over his eyes, but Sadie poked him. "It's your house," she said sleepily. "You go."

Jake grumbled but got out of bed. He pulled on a pair of jeans and ran his hand through his hair, then disappeared down the hallway towards the front door.

Sadie heard a greeting, then low, rumbling voices. Then she heard Jake exclaim, "dammit!" and she sat up straight, clutching the sheets to her bare chest. The door closed, and he came down the hallway, a piece of paper in his hand and an intense frown on his face.

"What is it?" Sadie's voice was tinged with worry.

"Fucking Royce Hensley," he said, putting the paper down on her bedside table and turning to the closet to get dressed. "There's a meeting in an hour."

Sadie didn't get it. She reached for the paper, squinting at it. It was probably time to transition to wearing glasses all the time, not just at her computer. Finally, it came into focus. It was a letter from the District Ranger, issuing a do not use the water notice for the Poplar housing complex based on test result inconsistencies.

"Oh man," Sadie said. "Even to shower?"

"Yep. We're not supposed to use it until they can get an independent tester."

"What does this have to do with Royce, though?"

Jake sat on the edge of the bed to pull on wool socks. "He did the water tests every month and reported the results. So this means he was doing it wrong, not doing it, or faking it, if the first month the test is done after his death, the results show we're not supposed to be using the water at all, much less drinking it."

Sadie grimaced. That was bad. That was real bad. She'd been hearing about water quality issues in the valley and surrounding areas for a while now. Agricultural runoff, combined with intense development and unreliable septic systems in the small amount of land available, had led to increased nitrate levels in the water table.

The water system at Hoback Junction, just upriver, was due for a total replacement and residents were working on forming a water district to pay for it while the federal government studied the problem. Sadie had to have drinking water delivered to the coffee kiosk until she could install a filtration system. Considering Poplar was just downriver, it wasn't surprising they were having similar issues.

"What kind of water problem is it?"

Jake shrugged, sighing. "That was the district engineer at the door handing out the notices. He didn't say exactly, just that the water was unfit for human use until they had further tests."

"Wow."

"Yeah. Want to come to the meeting with me? The Ranger is going to be there to answer questions."

Of course Sadie wanted to go. Plus, it would give her a chance to eye her suspects again. She felt the pull of worry, based on this morning's events, from the detective's warnings, but she pushed them aside. No one was going to tell Sadie "Nosy Bitch" Moose that she couldn't ask some questions. She wasn't afraid. And besides, she was just attending a meeting with her boyfriend. "Yeah," she said. "I was gonna shower, but I guess that's off limits. I'll get dressed." Jake leaned over and gave her a kiss, then got up and moved down the hallway.

"I'll make some tea."

# Chapter Nineteen

The meeting was held in the shop, a big corrugated metal building with large bay doors at the edge of the housing complex where the river rangers and fire crew worked in the summer. The floors had been swept and chairs were setup in a circle. An old heater droned on the wall, working unsuccessfully to heat the cold cement and metal space. Everyone kept their coats on as they came in and settled on the chairs. The mood was somber, and no one exchanged words as they sat and waited for the Ranger to arrive. A tall, lanky white man in his fifties with thinning hair wearing a dark green US Forest Service uniform stood at the door, greeting people as they arrived and handing out a packet of material. This was the district engineer, Sadie guessed.

Sadie sat next to Jake and peered over his shoulder at the material he was paging through. There were graphs with trend lines, and pages of small-typed words, information on the test results and what they meant. Jake seemed engrossed, so Sadie took the opportunity to observe the crowd.

Absent was Meadow, who Sadie remembered was working

from her boyfriend's house for awhile, and the three roommates, Sydney, Megan, and Travis. The people Sadie didn't recognize from Royce's memorial were there, and Sadie made a mental note to ask Jake their names. Cole was there, but Holly and little Violet weren't. He sat, arms crossed over his chest, face stern, not looking around. Elaina was wearing her uniform and paging through the documents with a worried look on her face. Darnell and Tamia huddled together, and it looked as though Tamia had been crying. Darnell wrapped an arm protectively around her. Jerry had declined to sit, and was standing against the workbench in the shop, glowering. Carl sat in a chair next to Elaina, the packet of papers in his lap unread. Justin was attending for DeeDee and family, and he sat on the other side of Elaina, glaring at the graph.

The door banged open, and everyone turned as a petite white woman with a sharp blonde bob and square framed lime green glasses burst into the room. She wore the same green uniform as the engineer, but brought a frenetic energy with her into the room. She was immediately talking, into the air, at no one and everyone at once.

"Oh, this is just awful, I'm so sorry for this but I'm so glad I could come and talk to everyone rest assured we're getting answers as quickly as possible and I brought a whole truckload of bottled water–" Sadie wasn't sure the woman had taken a breath since she entered the room, but she didn't seem to need it as she walked over to an empty chair and primly sat down on it, crossing her legs and leaning in to the circle with a sincere look on her face. "We just don't know what to think about this. We never would have imagined that something like this could happen, and I can assure you we're launching a full investigation, right Elaina?"

Elaina sat up straight. "Yes, ma'am, of course."

The woman laughed. "Don't call me ma'am, you know that, Elaina. Please, everyone, call me Doris." Doris looked around. "Now I don't know everyone, please, let's go around and introduce ourselves."

Sadie smothered a smile behind her hand and looked at Jake, who winked at her. This was the woman that inspired men to break apart their fistfights? To quake in their boots at the thought of having to meet with her? This was the Ranger everyone was so frightened of? Doris seemed more likely to bake Sadie cookies or volunteer to organize her pantry than reprimand her.

Everyone introduced themselves, and Sadie learned that the three folks she didn't know were in fact, residents of the Forest-owned tiny homes. When everyone said their names, Doris immediately greeted them and repeated their names back, adding anything that she knew about them, a recognizable tactic from Sadie's business school networking meetings. Also the same tactic Michael Scott used in *The Office*, often to hilarious results.

When Jake introduced himself, and then his girlfriend Sadie Moose, Doris's eyes grew wide behind her glasses and she sat up straight. "Sadie Moose! The famous baker! I just love your cinnamon rolls. The pumpkin is my favorite in the fall."

Sadie smiled and thanked her.

"How neat to meet you, I'm just tickled, Sadie Moose."

They moved on until everyone had introduced themselves to the Ranger.

"Now," she said, "let me explain what's happened. As you know, the dear departed Royce Hensley was in charge of doing the water tests down here. He did them every month and filed the results in our database as required. We started doing these monthly tests several years ago after Hoback Junction started having their water issues, and after reports that the water here tastes bad."

"It does," Cole said flatly. "Frankly, I don't think any of us drink it, even filtered." There were nods around the circle.

Doris nodded sympathetically. "We've heard those concerns, but the water tests came back every month well within the Environmental Protection Agency, public health, and Forest Service guidelines, so we thought it was simply a mineral issue that was causing the taste problems, not that there was anything unsafe about it."

"But now?" Darnell's voice was low and angry.

"When Thomas," Doris gestured at the district engineer, who'd sat beside her, "completed the test today on schedule, his results were immediately suspect. He completed the test two more times at the same source, then again at several residences. Each time, the results were far outside the acceptable range. He immediately let me know, then came back to the office and ran statistics on the results, which is the graph you have in front of you." Thomas handed Doris the packet, and she flipped to the graph and held it up.

"What you're seeing here is three years of test results. Each line tests a different water particle. You'll see that until today, the results were within the acceptable limits, indicated by the gray zone. They varied between two and four milligrams per liter. But today's results for nitrates jumped far, far, outside, by a hugely statistical margin. The EPA's safe drinking water threshold for nitrates is under ten milligrams per liter. Today Thomas found levels of nitrate ranging from forty-eight to fifty-two milligrams per liter."

Everyone examined the graph. Sadie noticed something else, too, and opened her mouth to speak before she could think better of it.

"Uh, Doris–" Sadie waited until Doris acknowledged her. "There's something funky about the graph before that, too."

Doris peered at the graph. "Do tell."

Sadie cleared her throat. "I imagine with this kind of test, it would be normal to have some fluctuations based on the season, water level, etcetera. This shows fluctuations, but the graph is like a perfect wave, the same repetition every six months. That seems like a statistical impossibility to me."

Doris turned the graph around to look at it, her lips pursed. Thomas cleared his throat, and she looked at him.

"You're right, Ms. Moose," he said in a soft voice. "I would expect to see more variability within the acceptable levels as well. I never looked at the trend line for more than a year, so it never stood out at me, but when I pulled up the long-term data, I saw that too."

"What does that mean?" Cole asked in a steely voice.

"Well...it would suggest that the same data is being inputted over and over again, in a cycle that shows short-term variability but not long term variability." Thomas said, his voice even.

There was silence for a moment, then a burst of angry voices.

"He was faking it?!"

"That rat bastard–"

"How could the Forest let one person be in charge–"

"I can't believe this–"

"Please, everyone," Doris said, and her quiet, bubbly voice suddenly took on an authority Sadie hadn't expected. This was the Ranger, it appeared. The voices quieted. "I hear your anger, frustration, and fear. I am going to sort this out. What Sadie pointed out and Thomas said is true. It appears that the data has been routinely manipulated, but we don't know why."

That quieted everyone down. Why would Royce fake the water tests? Sadie couldn't imagine a good reason.

"We're going to find out why, and what this means for the water system, and most importantly, for all of your health." Doris's voice had softened, but her resolve was clear. "From our understanding, the water should be fine as long as it's not consumed, but until we get an expert to clear that, we're asking you not use it at all."

"I'll want my own expert," Cole said, and there was a chorus of agreement in the crowd.

"That's understandable. You trusted us, you trusted *me* to keep you safe, and this was a breach of trust. I fully support you seeking second opinions. The data and information will be available to you."

Tamia suddenly sobbed, and Darnell wrapped her in his arms. There were tears in his eyes, too.

"Oh, dear," Doris said.

Darnell smoothed a hand over Tamia's back. Finally, he looked around the circle, then right at Doris. "We're expecting. We're both scared about what this might mean for our baby."

Sadie's heart squeezed. There was a chorus of murmurs, and Doris got up to comfort Tamia.

Justin cleared his throat. "We've been here a long time, and though we drink bottled water, we surely take a drink from the tap now and then and my boys are all okay."

Darnell nodded at him.

Finally, Doris turned away from the Bells to address everyone else. "This is on me, and I want you each to know that I will make this right. I'm going to ask for patience, and, this is going to be hard, discretion. We're sharing this information with the investigators that are investigating Royce's death. We think it's important to keep it within Poplar if we can, at least until Royce's killer has been brought to justice."

Elaina, who had been silent the entire meeting, spoke up

then. "I've sent this information to Detective Nolan. He's asking for prudence as well."

Carl cleared his throat, and Sadie looked at him for the first time. He looked stricken. Her mind suddenly went to the tremendous loss he had just suffered, and her heart ached for him. Was it possible his wife's cancer had been related to these water quality issues? "I will be quiet about it," he said finally. Then he got up and left.

Everyone watched him go, Elaina with a thoughtful look on her face, everyone else looking sad. After that, the meeting broke up. Jake helped Doris deliver gallons of water, along with packets of information on the resources being made available to everyone at Poplar, to each house. Sadie studied the information inside, standing next to the roaring wood stove and trying to warm her cold behind. The Forest had a number to call to set up testing and physicals at no cost to the employee and a contact for mental health counseling. They'd set up an agreement with two gyms for Poplar residents to shower for free, and they were working on getting a heated mobile shower truck to park on the compound until they had the all clear to use the water for bathing. All things considered, it seemed to Sadie that the agency was responding well to this crisis.

She heard Jake's boots on the porch and turned to the door as he came in. His face was blank. Sadie wrapped her arms around him, laying her head on his chest. His arms came around her and he sighed deeply.

"Hey," she said, "let's go to my place for your days off."

"Yeah," Jake said. "I could use a break."

As Jake packed a bag, Sadie looked out the window at the darkening neighborhood. Lights burned in windows, smoke curled from chimneys. Sadie imagined everyone reading the information they'd been provided, adjusting to the idea of using bottled water for everything from drinking to cooking to brushing their teeth, and her heart ached for them. Then she remembered that the person who had perpetuated this harm on the community was dead, and a cold tendril of dread swept through her. She'd been asking why anyone would kill Royce now, when he'd always been a pain in the ass, and now she might have an answer.

# Chapter Twenty

Jake followed Sadie into town. With his headlights steady behind her, she let her mind drift as she drove the familiar stretch of highway. What did it all mean? It had been less than a week since Royce's murder. What did Sadie really know?In the weeks prior to his death, Royce had been seen arguing with several neighbors, but they all pointed fingers at each other instead of owning up to it. Darnell saw him and DeeDee argue. DeeDee saw him and Meadow argue. Meadow saw Royce argue with someone that looked like Preston Chandler. DeeDee knew the three roommates were mad at Royce, but the three roommates had seen Cole confront Royce. Sadie herself had seen him and Jerry go at it. By everyone's account, he'd been causing trouble for years, and these sorts of confrontations were normal, though. So why would someone kill him now?

On the day of his death, he'd been in a fistfight in a public place with Jerry. Cole had been there to break it up. Were they together? Sadie needed more details about that confrontation. She realized, suddenly, that she hadn't ever talked to Cole, just Holly. She needed to track him down, ask him about that morning, and ask about the private inholding he managed. Something about that tickled Sadie's brain, but she couldn't figure out why.

The afternoon of the fight, Meadow had seen someone Sadie presumed to be Preston Chandler come to Royce's door, and Royce hadn't been happy to see him there. Had Royce made a plan to meet with Preston later at the hot springs? Why there, of all places? What were Preston's connections to the area? What did they have to argue about? What was Preston's deal, anyway? She'd gotten distracted and hadn't looked him up earlier.

When Sadie and Jake arrived at the hot springs, a snowmobile had been there. Sadie needed to ask Jake if he'd recognized it as Royce's. She remembered at the time he'd given it a second look. And why had Royce been falsifying the water test results, and for so long? It seemed so malicious. Nitrates could really impact the health of his neighbors. And him! Even if he drank only bottled water, he still used the water to bathe and wash dishes. Why would he risk that? Was he doing it to cover his own ass? Had he made a mistake and not been able to own up to it?

And what had happened to Amos? The detective had confirmed he hadn't been drunk. What had caused him to black out? Would he eventually remember something more, or was his memory going to be missing forever? Sadie needed to do some more research into what could knock a person out. Chloroform, roofies...some other drug?

Whoever had murdered Royce, Sadie must have interacted with them. Otherwise, why would someone break into her coffee kiosk, destroy it, and paint the words 'nosy bitch' on it? Something about the paint bothered Sadie, too. Such a distinctive color. And it had been thick, heavy paint, not the same as the spray paint she was used to using. There was probably something there she needed to figure out, among so many other things.

Sadie caught sight of brake lights in front of her, and she slowed. She was in the narrow section of road after Hoback Junction, before the road entered the Jackson valley, the Hole of Jackson Hole. On her right was a sheer cliff face, and on the left was the long, steep slope down to the Snake River below. It was common to see deer and elk on the road along this section. She glanced in her rearview mirror and frowned. Jake's headlights were gone. Had he pulled off at the Junction? Did he need gas?

She slowed further as the brake lights in front of her flashed again.

*What was going on?*

Headlights caught her rearview mirror, and she squinted. Someone was behind her again, but they were moving quickly. She gripped the steering wheel tightly and checked her speed. She was going under the speed limit, spooked by the brake lights. Were there elk on the road ahead? Hitting one would total her Subaru. She kept her speed slow and steady, and the headlights grew closer.

They were so bright they were blinding. She tilted her rearview mirror so they wouldn't shine in her eyes, quickly bringing her eyes back to the road. It was only a mile or so more through the narrow section, then whoever was behind her could pass if they wanted to drive so fast. Let them hit the elk in the road, not her.

"Jeez, get off my ass," Sadie murmured grumpily. Whoever this was, they were riding her bumper. If she had to brake quickly, they were both goners.

Resolutely, Sadie kept her eyes ahead. Her headlights illuminated the last curve in the road before it opened up. As she negotiated the turn, she saw elk in the road, her lights flashing on their dark rumps and wide dark eyes.

She braked, hard, to avoid hitting the herd, keeping the wheel pointed straight.

Swerving could be deadly.

But at as she was braking, her tires caught a bit of ice on the road, and her car slid sideways, narrowly missing the elk but ramming into the snowy ditch. The truck that had been behind her roared by, not slowing, barely missing the elk as they bolted.

Sadie sat, breathing hard. She dropped her head back onto the headrest to take a deep breath. She'd already had one panic attack today. She didn't need to have another. Slowly, she took stock. She was fine. She'd been braking when she'd hit the ice and hadn't been going very fast to begin with. Her Subaru had gone into the ditch, but luckily there was three feet of snow piled up over the guard rail, so she hadn't impacted hard. She needed to get out, check her vehicle, and see if she could drive it away. No cars had passed since the asshole behind her had gone by—without checking on her, which made her think it wasn't a local. Wyoming hospitality would dictate you check on someone when they go off the road. She flipped on her hazard lights, pulled on her mittens and hat, and pushed her door open with effort, getting out of the car.

With one look, Sadie realized she wasn't driving her car away. Her front bumper had impacted the snowbank and was buried in the snow. The car was at an angle off the road and her back tires weren't even on the ground. She was nosed in, and without the back tires for traction, she was stuck there. She groaned. There wasn't cell service on this part of the highway, so she'd need to wait until someone came along. Jake should be right behind her. Even if he'd stopped for fuel, he had to be back on the road by now. Sadie glanced up and down the highway. She wasn't in a great spot. Anyone coming around the bend wouldn't see her until they were negotiating the corner. She'd be safest in her car.

She was turning to wrench her door open when headlights swept across her. She threw her arm up to block the blinding light. *Turn off your brights, asshole*, Sadie thought.

Then she heard a gunning engine, and a squeal of tires, and she realized they were headed right for her.

* * *

Sadie threw herself onto the hood of her car, sliding across the Subaru and landing against the snow drift. She put her arms over her head and braced for impact. It never came, though, and she forced herself to open her eyes, glimpsing taillights on a dark-colored, lifted truck going around the corner right before Jake's truck pulled in behind her.

"What the hell, Sadie, are you okay?" Jake yelled, getting out of his truck and running over to her.

Sadie's breath was sawing in and out of her chest.

"What happened?" Jake reached a hand across the hood of the car to help her back across.

"I...I hit some ice trying to avoid elk and ended up here."

"Why are you on your hood, though?" Jake slid her over to him and pulled her to her feet, steadying her.

"This is going to sound nuts, but I swear that truck that just passed you was aiming for me when they came around the corner."

Jake swallowed hard and pulled her into his chest, wrapping his arms tight around her. "It doesn't sound nuts. You've pissed someone off. I should have told you I needed to stop for gas and we could've stopped together."

"It's okay," Sadie said into his chest.

"It's not. I promised to protect you, and I'm doing a shitty job of it."

Sadie wrapped her arms around Jake and held him to her, hard. "It really is okay, Jake. I'm okay, and you're here now."

They were silent for a moment longer, then Jake pulled away from her to look at her car. "I can get that out, I think."

Jake was, of course, able to get her car out. It was a little tricky being on the corner, but he hooked the Subaru's back axle to a come-along at the front of his truck and pulled it out of the ditch by backing carefully up the side of the road. When they had the Subaru on all four tires, they walked around it. The front bumper had a slight dent, but otherwise it seemed no worse for wear. Promising he would stay right behind her, Jake undid the tow line and climbed into the truck, and the two of them pulled out onto the highway, proceeding slowly into town.

* * *

Later that night, Sadie and Jake sat in front of the fire in her living room, cuddled up on one of the couches Sadie couldn't bring herself to replace. They were ugly, but they were comfortable. Tyrone lay at their feet, snoring. The remains of the dinner they'd picked up at Get Rich or Thai Tryin', their favorite local food truck, was spread out on the coffee table in front of them.

Jake coughed and took a sip of his beer. "Malee is not fucking around with level five spice."

Sadie laughed. "That she is not."

She snuggled in closer to him. She didn't want to think about the case, about almost getting run over on a dark highway, about the ruins of her coffee kiosk with the nasty message scrawled for all to see, but she knew she needed to.

"That night at the hot springs, Jake," she started, "did you recognize that snowmobile as Royce's?"

Jake took another drink of his beer. "Yes and no?"

"Explain."

"Royce had just gotten a brand new sled this year. Fancy thing, must've set him back over $15k. I'd seen him on it on the compound. The snowmobile that was up at the hot springs was his old one. I didn't know if he'd sold it, or if it was just one that looked like it. I would've recognized his new one right away, but I couldn't tell if the old one was his or not."

"So when you saw the body, though..."

"Right." Jake cleared his throat again. "When I saw the body, and thought about the snowmobile, and where we were... it made me think it was Royce."

Sadie was silent for a moment.

"Why do you think Royce would fake those test results?"

"I have no idea." Jake's voice was hard. "But he's more of a bastard than I thought. When I think of Tamia and Darnell, worried about their baby, and the Coxes, with their three kids, and Chase and Holly with little Violet...And the dogs! All the dogs probably drink tap water. I can't believe he'd be that irresponsible."

Sadie frowned, thinking of Tyrone. "Who told you to drink bottled water when you moved in?"

Jake blinked at her. "Uh...shit. Actually, Royce did."

"What did he say, exactly?"

Jake ran his hand over his face. "He said the water didn't taste good, so everyone drank bottled. He recommended buying the big five gallon jugs with the dispenser at the store, then refilling them from the natural spring on the way to the hot springs or in town at the office."

They both sat with that information for a while. So Royce had faked the water tests and told residents to drink bottled or natural spring water. What did that mean, that he was both causing harm and trying to reduce harm?

"Did you ever see Royce with Preston Chandler?"

"Who?"

"He's a developer. Drives a new black Mercedes G-Wagon, wears fancy boots even in the snow, ten gallon hat?"

Jake's face cleared of confusion. "Oh. I didn't know his name, but yeah. I think he's involved with the development across the river from Poplar. The multi-million dollar home sites? It's funny to be paying reasonable rent across the way from them."

"On the other side of the red bridge?"

"Yeah."

"Huh." Sadie's mind wanted to connect some dots there, but she found she couldn't. "He wanted to meet with Paige about a land swap, swapping some land near the junction with the fairgrounds parcel."

Jake made a face. "That sounds advantageous to him and no one else."

"That's what I thought. Paige said it would never happen. But did you see Royce with him?"

"No, but I've seen him around at the Junction. At the market and stuff. He's not doing a great job of selling those home sites. They're spendy, hard to access across that bridge, and too far from town for the price."

Sadie considered that. "Meadow said that the day Royce was murdered, Preston came to Royce's house, and Royce wasn't happy to see him. Meadow thinks they set up a time to meet later."

"Like Preston was meeting with Royce up at the hot springs?"

"Yeah."

Jake looked skeptical. "I never saw him on a snowmobile."

"Is the trip up to the hot springs hard, though? You groom it."

"It isn't hard, true. And he could have some sort of tracked UTV, those are a nice ride."

Tyrone stood then and put his head in Sadie's lap. She scratched his soft brown ears and fuzzy snout. He looked up at her with his big, brown, moose-like eyes...and farted.

"Ewwwww," Sadie groaned. "Okay, out with you."

She got up to let Tyrone out, and Jake cleaned up their leftovers. It wasn't late, but they were both exhausted. Sadie needed to open the bakery at 3:30 a.m., so they retired to bed soon after.

# Chapter Twenty-One

The next morning, Sadie covered the counter while Jorge took his break. Kendall was at the coffee kiosk, supervising the window glass installers. After they finished, Jake was going to help replace the door and change the locks, as well as experiment with a few different ways to remove the paint.

The pre-ski crowd had thinned, so when Elaina stepped into the bakery with an older woman and teenager in tow, Sadie noticed them immediately.

"Hey, Elaina," Sadie said in greeting.

Elaina moved towards the counter, ushering her guests with her. "Sadie, this is Lauren, and her son, Dylan."

Sadie greeted them with a smile. Lauren was in her early fifties, with graying hair pulled back in a braid under a knit hat. She was white, with wrinkles around her blue eyes. She looked grim. Her son was taller than her, a lanky teenager with long limbs, sandy hair, and dark, sullen eyes. He didn't look right at her.

"Lauren is Royce's ex-wife," Elaina said finally, after the two didn't introduce themselves.

"Oh," Sadie said. Her voice grew soft. "I'm so sorry for your loss, Lauren and Dylan."

Dylan scoffed and rolled his eyes, a patented move Sadie remembered from her own teenage years. "Not like it's any big loss to me," he muttered.

"Dylan," Lauren said sharply. She put a hand on his arm. "Royce and I divorced when Dylan was a toddler. He didn't know him very well."

Sadie felt for the teenager. He was radiating indifference, but he hadn't known his father well, and now he would never get the chance. It might not bother him now, but if it did in the future, there was nothing he could do about it. What a cruel twist.

"They're here to take care of Royce's house." Elaina peered into the glass bakery case.

"That sounds like a big job," Sadie said. She turned and picked up a bakery box off the back counter. "Help me pick out a few things you'd like to take along with you, for fuel."

"Oh," Lauren said, looking surprised. "That's kind of you." She paused. "Did you know Royce?"

Sadie didn't want to tell her she'd been the one to find his body.

"Just in passing," she said finally. "My boyfriend Jake lives at Poplar as well."

Lauren's expression grew guarded again.

Elaina cleared her throat. "Sadie and Jake were up at the hot springs that night, Lauren," she said softly. "They're not suspects."

Lauren's eyes snapped to Sadie's and her mouth formed an O. "Oh," she said knowingly. "Dylan, pick out some pastries. Then maybe you and Elaina can go check out the antler arches on the town square. I want to talk to Sadie."

* * *

Sadie sat down with Lauren with trepidation. What did the woman want with her?

Lauren sipped the tea Sadie had poured for her, and Sadie sipped a cup of coffee with cream and sugar. They were silent for a moment.

"I heard you were asking questions about Royce's murder," Lauren said finally, and Sadie almost choked on her coffee.

After sputtering for a minute, she took a breath to reply. "Uh...where'd you hear that?"

"From DeeDee Cox."

"Oh. Do you know DeeDee from when you lived at Poplar? Oh, wait. Did you live at Poplar?"

"Yes. Royce and I picked out that mobile home together." Lauren took a sip of tea.

"When was the last time you were here?"

"I left with Dylan when he was three. So almost...twelve years ago. DeeDee and Justin moved in a year after us. We knew them as a young couple before they had any babies. We kept in touch. I shop her makeup sales."

Sadie thought about that. "Then you know Royce was on her about running her business out of the compound?"

"I do. And I wasn't surprised. Royce was a real sonofabitch. And I've met his mother, so that's saying something."

Sadie suppressed a laugh. It seemed wrong, still, to be joking about the dead.

"That probably seems crass of me," Lauren said, looking down into her teacup. "But that man was never easy to live with, and he was a piss poor father to Dylan. Never sent a cent of child support until I sent the government after him and they took it out of his checks. That is..."

"That is?"

"Until recently. In the last few years, Royce started sending big checks to me, telling me to sock them away for Dylan's college fund."

Sadie frowned. "Did he get a promotion? A raise?"

Lauren looked outside, then back at Sadie. "No. He's been in the same position since I left him. He's gotten regular longevity increases, but it doesn't account for it."

"Did he win the lottery? Sell a patent? Make money off investments? Play the meme stock market game?"

Lauren pursed her lips. "I can't say that he didn't do any of those things. He wouldn't tell me where the money came from."

"Did you tell DeeDee about it?"

"No. But she mentioned to me he was driving a new truck, and had gotten a new snowmobile."

Sadie thought about that. Jake had mentioned Royce's new snowmobile just last night.

"Why are you telling me about it, Lauren?"

"DeeDee told me about the water tests last night. Maybe someone was paying Royce to fake them."

Sadie's eyes widened. "That's definitely a theory. I've been puzzling over why he would do that, too. But who would benefit from the tests being faked enough to pay off Royce?"

"I don't know. But I wanted you to have that information. Dylan and I are going down there today to sort through things. If I can get access to his banking information, I'll let you know what I find out."

* * *

Jake called as Sadie left the bakery headed to the police station to give her fingerprints. The lunch rush was over, and Jorge, Max, and Sage could handle closing and prep for the next day. Sadie wanted get this errand done, then throw the ball for

Tyrone in the backyard and think on what she'd learned so far about the case. She also needed to sit down and look at the financials behind expanding the coffee kiosks like she and Kendall had talked about. The idea had implanted itself in Sadie's brain, and despite the setback at Hoback Junction, she could see how it was a good idea. It would stretch her leadership abilities, her finances, and her need for control to bring on a partner, but she trusted Kendall implicitly. Plus, if this would keep Kendall around, she'd be a fool not to jump on it.

Sadie swiped her finger across the screen to answer Jake's call.

"Hello gorgeous," she said cheerily. It was a cloudless, blue sky day. The snow was perfect on the mountains, the air was crisp and clean, and Sadie had the afternoon off. What wasn't there to be cheery about?

"Hello to you too, sunshine," Jake laughed.

"How's my kiosk looking?"

"Almost like new. New door, new windows, new locks. I got the paint off with the pressure washer. That stuff wasn't regular spray paint."

"I wondered."

"I have a theory, but I'd rather tell you in person."

"Then I'll look forward to seeing your cute booty at my house later."

"Actually, I was hoping you'd come back to Poplar tonight? I know we said we'd stay there, but you don't have to open the bakery tomorrow, and your espresso guy is going to be here early."

Sadie considered. "Can I bring Tyrone?"

"I would be upset if you didn't. I didn't buy that dog bed for anyone but him."

"Okay. Why not. I'll pack a bag and bring Tyrone down."

"And beer?"

"And beer."

"And dinner?"

"You drive a hard bargain, Mr. Moreno, but you're on."

"And Sadie?"

"Yeah?"

"Watch your back on the drive. Get on the road before dark. Call me when you leave."

# Chapter Twenty-Two

Sadie's drive to Poplar was uneventful, though she kept her eyes on her rearview mirror the entire drive, watching for a lifted truck with a grudge. On the way, she stopped at her coffee kiosk to survey the work her crew had done. Just like Jake said, the paint had come off, leaving no trace of the message. The new windows gleamed under the locked shutters they'd had installed for an extra layer of protection. The new door had extra reinforcement, and her security cameras had been replaced and moved to give full coverage. It was locked up tight, cleaned up inside, and ready for the espresso machine repairer to fix her beloved Francesca. They'd be back in business by Saturday. Or Monday. Maybe she'd have the murder solved by then, and they'd be able to reopen without worrying about reprisal.

Poplar was quiet when she pulled into Jake's driveway. The sky was clear, and the temperature had dropped into the single digits. The weather report said a big storm was moving in the next afternoon, and eyeing the giant snow piles around the compound, Sadie wondered where they would put it all. As she got out of the car and Tyrone jumped out, she eyed the circle of houses. Lights were on, smoke, as always, puffing out of the chimneys. Vehicles were parked in front of most of them.

Sadie remembered the lifted truck that had tried to run her over and scanned the houses for it. She snorted. Almost every house had a truck in front of it, including Jake's. Cole drove a lifted black truck. Jerry drove a tan truck. Justin drove a lifted black truck. There were Forest Service vehicles in front of the houses of Elaina and Carl. Sadie wondered if they had personal vehicles, and if they ever drove them home. Sadie spotted a small four-door sedan in front of Royce's house, and realized the lights and wood stove were on there, too. She thought of Lauren and Dylan going through Royce's things, and hoped they were finding some solace in the action.

"Coming in?" a deep voice asked on the porch, and Tyrone let out a joyous bark as he ran up the stairs to greet Jake.

"Yeah," Sadie said, shaking off her thoughts and reaching into the Subaru to grab the grocery and overnight bags she'd brought. She shut the door and turned to Jake. He was dressed in a red flannel and jeans, looking as sturdy, steadfast, and handsome as the Brawny lumberjack. She grinned and headed up the stairs. Jake put out his arms to take her bags, but she walked into them instead.

"I hope you're not too hungry," she whispered in his ear, then caught the lobe between her teeth in a playful nip. "I think I want you as my first course."

After a long first course in the bedroom and a late dinner of chicken parmesan, Sadie and Jake sat entwined on the couch in his living room, watching the roaring wood stove while NPR played in the background, Tyrone at their feet.

"Okay," Sadie said. "Tell me your theory, finally."

"First—did you see the detective today when you got your fingerprints taken?"

Sadie frowned and took a sip of her wine. "I didn't. I was in and out pretty quickly."

"Okay. He was down here again today, poking around Royce's house."

Sadie processed that information, wondering what the detective might have found.

"Anyway, have you ever heard of tree marking paint?" Jake asked.

"Nope."

"Right. Ever been in the woods and seen trees with paint on them? Sometimes symbols, sometimes bands or lines?"

Sadie thought about it.

"Yes, actually. I always wondered what they meant."

"Well, they're put there by foresters, usually, or loggers, to mark keep trees or boundaries during a logging or thinning operation."

"Okay..."

"Well, regular spray paint doesn't absorb well into tree bark, and you have to be pretty close to use it, so foresters use a special kind of paint. It's an aerosol, but it's thicker and sprays out further so they don't have to be as close to the trees to be accurate."

"And I'm guessing that's the kind of paint you think was used on my kiosk?"

"Bingo."

Sadie thought about that. "Is powder blue a common tree marking paint color?"

Jake shrugged. "The colors rarely mean the same thing from unit to unit."

"You sure know a lot about this. I thought your job was to put fires out."

"It is. But in the shoulder seasons, we all work on fuels reduction to make fires less intense. I've also worked for a logging company before, back in college...when I went to forestry school."

Sadie laughed. "Oh right. I forgot about that."

"So have I," Jake said, deadpan.

They were silent for a moment. Sadie ran her foot over Tyrone's back below her. "So who do we know that would have access to that kind of paint?"

"Well, that's where it gets tricky. Anyone could buy it at a supply store in town, or online. And anyone with access to the shop could grab a can."

"Do you have access to the shop?"

"Yep."

"So it could be anyone at Poplar? Not much of a clue, then."

"Well...that's true. But there is one forester here on the loop, which I think makes him a more likely suspect."

"Oh! Jerry, right?"

"Yep. Jerry."

Sadie made a face. "I still think it's too obvious for it to be him. What about Preston Chandler? Do you think he could get a hold of tree paint?"

Jake barked out a laugh. "Preston Chandler doesn't do dirty work. If he's behind this, I can almost guarantee he paid someone to do it for him."

"Sounds like someone else I know," Sadie said, thinking of Claire Cabot, Kendall's billionaire girlfriend with dubious connections to the Chicago mob. Her assistant, Sully, and driver, Baxter, did all her dirty work for her—from following people to running her dry cleaning. Sadie perked up. "Actually, I don't know why I didn't think of that before!" She pulled her phone out of her leggings pocket and opened her contacts, scrolling down to find Claire's name.

"Think of what?"

"Claire Cabot probably knows something about Preston Chandler. What doesn't she know? He's probably a competitor of hers, anyway." Claire ran the land development arm of her family's business. Despite Sadie's initial doubts on Claire's intentions, she'd proven that she was trying to do good with the money instead of just get richer. She was currently working on building deed-restricted workforce housing up near the resort. Sadie pressed the call button, glancing at the clock. It was a little after nine o'clock, not too late to call. She got voicemail immediately, though. Sighing, Sadie flipped over to a text message.

`Hey Claire. Call me when you can? Wondering about Preston Chandler.`

Sadie watched for the three dots that would show Claire was typing, but didn't see them. She'd have to wait to hear from her then.

Tyrone's ears perked up, and Sadie suddenly heard barking outside, followed by a yell. Jake's head snapped toward the door, and he jumped up to lift the blinds from the door. "Oh shit," he said, his voice shocked.

Sadie bolted up to look over his shoulder. His gaze was directed at Royce Hensley's house. And it was on fire.

* * *

The next few minutes were a whirlwind of activity. Jake shoved his feet into boots and put on his coat and gloves as he flew out the door. Sadie called 911, who'd said they'd already been alerted, then put on her own boots and winter layers to go out to see if she could help.

The first thing that struck Sadie was the sound. She didn't know fire could be so loud. It roared, the sound of oxygen and material being consumed filling the night air. Flames shot out the roof, orange sparks flying and dark ash raining down to disturb the white snow. A cluster of hastily clad residents stood back from the house, clutching one another. Sadie scanned the faces, immediately relieved to see the shocked faces of Lauren and Dylan among the crowd. Elaina hovered near them, looking around at her neighbors suspiciously. DeeDee was crying. Carl stood off to the side, staring at the flames, blank faced. The three roommates were huddled together, arms wrapped around one another. Meadow was of course absent, as was Jerry. Cole, Darnell, Justin, and Jake were digging out the nearest fire hydrant from the snow that had piled up. Sadie made her way to Lauren and Dylan.

"Are you okay?" She asked.

Lauren's stunned eyes traveled slowly to her face.

"We're...okay," she said after a time. She looked at Dylan as if to confirm it.

"We are okay, Mom," he said, wrapping an arm around her. His eyes were wide, his mouth set firmly.

"What happened?"

Elaina looked at Sadie sharply, then at Lauren. "I should ask, actually, Sadie," Elaina said. "What happened, Lauren?"

"We were in the kitchen..." she trailed off.

"We were in the kitchen and we heard a loud noise on the roof," Dylan said. "The next thing we knew, we smelled smoke, and we came outside and saw the flames."

"Yes," Lauren said, nodding. "That's what happened."

Elaina eyed them both, but they heard sirens, so she started clearing them away from the house, which was now fully engulfed. The Hoback Volunteer Fire Department trucks pulled in where they had been standing, and everyone watched from their viewpoint down the street, out of the way. A light snow fell. Jake came up next to her and put an arm around her.

Sadie leaned into his comforting strength. He was puffing from the exertion and the shock.

"Won't be anything left," Carl said, suddenly. "These trailers...they just go up when they catch."

DeeDee gasped. "You shouldn't say that, Carl."

"It's true."

"We hadn't gone through much," Lauren said, her voice weepy. "Now we won't have the chance."

"We didn't need anything of his, anyway," Dylan said.

They stood silently, watching the firefighters hook up their hoses and start battling the fire. As the flames soared for the sky, an oily, greasy odor filled the air. Sadie watched the ash fall and wondered if the last evidence that would bring Royce's murderer to justice was falling down on her.

# Chapter Twenty-Three

The espresso guy was late and cranky when he finally showed up. He viewed Sadie's battered Francesca with empathy in his eyes though, running his hand over the dents and broken knobs and crooning that he'd make her all better. Sadie left him to his work and trudged across the parking lot to the market to wait.

Halfway across, she realized there was a vehicle right behind her, creeping. She scooted closer to the parked cars, having a déjà vu moment of when Carl had talked to her in this parking lot. She thought about what he'd said last night as they watched Royce's house burn. Was it just an observation, if an ill-timed one? Or had it had more devious implications? The police had searched Royce's house after he was found. Surely they would've found anything that would implicate his murderer? Sadie remembered what Lauren had said about Royce suddenly having a lot of money. Had the police looked at his bank statements? Had Lauren? She hadn't asked her last night. Once the firefighters were underway, the local sheriff had arrived to question everyone, and once Sadie and Jake had said their piece, they'd been ordered back into Jake's house. Sadie wasn't even sure where Lauren and Dylan were at this point.

The vehicle was still inching behind her, and Sadie felt a shiver of fear. It was broad daylight, in a semi-busy parking lot. This wasn't the time to be threatening her, right? With a deep breath, she whirled around to confront whoever was following her. It was a new black SUV, and as she turned, the back window rolled down.

"Didn't mean to spook you, Sadie," a clear, feminine voice said. "But you said you needed to talk?"

Sadie sighed in relief and approached the window. "You shouldn't sneak up on me like that, Claire. And you too, Bax and Sully."

Baxter looked at her ruefully from the driver's seat. "You were lost in thought when we spotted you." He was a giant of a man, a former NFL linebacker, with copper skin and black hair. The first time Kendall had seen him, he'd intimidated even her, but they'd since become good friends.

"You should pay more attention to your surroundings," Sully said from the front passenger seat. As tall as Baxter but rail thin, Sully was white, with a long oval face and a crooked nose. His voice was high and nasally. He sported a bruise on his cheek, and Sadie raised an eyebrow at him. He touched it and winced painfully. "Caught a tip and yard-saled," he explained. Sadie gave a murmur of empathy. Sully had decided he wanted to learn to ski and was taking lessons at the big resort. A yard sale meant he'd fallen and his skis had popped off and poles had gone flying. It happened to every beginner, and could be painful.

"I want to take you for a drive," Claire said, interrupting Sadie's thoughts. Sadie glanced back at her coffee kiosk.

"I can't be gone too long," she said.

"We don't need to go far."

Sadie shrugged and climbed in the back with Claire and buckled up. Claire was white, with straight blonde hair and hazel eyes. She was petite and graceful. Her small stature and classic good looks masked the shrewd businesswoman she was.

"Where are we headed?"

Baxter pointed the SUV south towards Poplar, Pritchard Hot Springs, and the Canyon.

"You asked about Preston Chandler."

"I did."

"I think it would be easier to show you what I know about Preston instead of telling you," Claire said. She took a sip from a stainless steel coffee tumbler.

Sadie peered out the front window. They were traveling towards the red bridge, where Preston Chandler had land on the other side. Fine. She could wait and see what Claire wanted her to see.

Silence filled the car.

"So, Sully, followed anyone lately?"

Sully let out a short bark of laughter. "Not lately, Ms. Moose."

"Hmph. What about you, Baxter? Claire have you up to any nefarious deeds?"

Claire rolled her eyes at her and looked out the window.

"Not recently, Sadie. I went ice fishing last week though. Heck of a thing."

Baxter regaled her with details of his ice fishing adventure for the rest of the drive, his enthusiasm dwindling as they turned to cross the red bridge over the Snake River just before reaching Poplar. Once they crossed, they continued along the road, not turning into Astoria, the commercial hot springs that had opened last summer. A few cars were in the parking lot, and Sadie could see mist rising from the pools behind the main building. She wondered when she'd be up for going into a hot spring again after last week. She wondered if Pritchard Hot Springs would reopen soon. It had been a week.

They continued along the road, curving around the bend of the Snake River, until the road cut back into the trees and the highway and river fell out of view. They climbed a grade, then dipped down, and a housing development popped into view. The lots were far apart, with natural barriers in place to preserve the scenic view of each and keep prying eyes out. There were only a few houses built so far.

"This is the Chandler Estates development," Claire said finally as they drove through a large stone gate. "Preston Chandler inherited this land from his father and started developing it a few years ago remotely. He's recently come into town full time after being unhappy with the sales of his parcels."

"Why haven't they been selling?" The area was beautiful, treed, with rocky outcroppings everywhere. The view of the mountains was extraordinary. The location was only twenty-five minutes from the town of Jackson, with the Snake River just below to launch rafts and fishing boats. Why wouldn't those with money to spend want to live here?

Baxter continued down the road, past the last of the development, onto what looked like a service road.

"The price is pretty steep for so far out of town, and getting materials and household goods across the red bridge is intensive. It's one reason people like it, of course. It's exclusive. But Preston hasn't lived up to the promise of the development. He sold this as a sporting club, with a golf course, clubhouse, and access to heli-skiing and river sports. But he ran out of money before he could put in those things, and he's relying on selling the lots to get there. It's a cycle."

The road curved around and Baxter came to a stop in front of a gate. Behind it was a vista of scrubby, cleared land with flagged metal stakes scattered around.

"This is the site for the golf course," Claire said, gesturing.

"Huh," Sadie said. "Seems weird to me to want to buy a house out here for the scenery, but also have access to a golf course."

"Rich people, man," Baxter commiserated from the front seat. His eyes snapped to Claire's, and she shrugged.

"You're right, Baxter. Here's the mystery, though..."

Sadie looked around like she expected the answer to pop up in the deserted landscape. "What?"

"Why hasn't he been able to put in the golf course? From what I know of his finances, he should've been able to fulfill this promise. What else is he spending money on?"

"Ohhhh," Sadie whispered. "I wonder...if they have water quality issues, too?"

"The whole development is on a fancy water filtration system," Claire said. "That was something he added after the initial wells had been dug. Cost a fortune."

Sadie pondered that. "Have there been water tests done on this side of the river that show the water isn't safe?" Sadie filled Claire in on the test results from Poplar and the issues they were currently facing.

"That's horrible," Claire said. "I don't know about that." She looked thoughtful. Baxter turned the car around, and they headed back out. As they neared the gate, she told him to pull into the model home by the entrance.

"Why?" Sadie asked, looking at Claire with confusion.

"Well, you have a question. Let's find out."

* * *

Sadie hadn't expected to play Claire Cabot's doting wife today, but then again, she hadn't expected a number of things recently. And if she was going to pretend to be a lesbian for mystery reasons, she couldn't ask for a more charming wife, really.

When they got out of the SUV and Claire tucked her hand into Sadie's arm, Sadie panicked a little.

"Should we have a backstory?"

"We're just going to ask about the development and work our way around to the water issues, Sadie," Claire said calmly. "They don't need our life story."

"We met at a roller derby match."

Claire smirked. "Was I skating or you?"

"Neither," Sadie said. "Unless you skate?"

"Of course I skate." They reached the doors. "You don't skate? Even ice skate? You're a Jackson Hole girl!"

"I haven't ice skated since I was a girl, but I'm talking roller skating."

"Right. Well, either way, I doubt it will come up."

"I sleep on the left side," Sadie whispered, and Claire chuckled.

Sadie's heart pounded as she opened the door for Claire, then ducked in behind her. The model home was a large, modern cabin. They stepped into a foyer with a pitched ceiling. A gentle bell jingled to announce their arrival, and they heard the clicking of heels on hardwood moving towards them from the back of the house.

"Act natural, Sadie," Claire hissed, looking at Sadie with alarm. "You're supposed to be the sleuthing pro."

Right. Sadie took a deep breath and pasted the rich and bored look Claire had settled her features into onto her own face. At least, she hoped she looked rich and bored, not constipated.

A woman walked down the hall towards them. She was dressed in a tailored forest green pantsuit and towering black stilettos. Her black hair cascaded over her shoulders in soft waves, and her makeup was flawless. She looked like a beauty pageant contestant, not a realtor. She beamed at them.

"Hello," she said. "Welcome to Chandler Estates. I'm Erica." She held out her hand and Sadie and Claire both shook it.

"I'm Claire, and this is my wife Sadie," Claire said smoothly. She peered around. "We're shopping around, so we thought we'd come by."

"Oh, how wonderful! Are you moving to the area?"

Sadie's mind blanked.

"Yes, from Chicago," Claire said seamlessly.

"That's a change of pace," Erica said. "Please, have a look around, and when you're ready, step into this front office and I can answer the questions you have. I'll pull together a packet of information for you. Everything you see in the house is customizable, and this is one of ten different floor plans we have available. Can I get you a coffee or tea?"

"No thanks," Claire said, and she strode off down the hall. Sadie smiled at Erica, hoping she didn't show too much teeth, then followed Claire.

The house was beautiful. Sadie had to give that to Preston Chandler. It was contemporary, with gleaming exposed dark wood beams, white walls, and matte stainless fixtures with clean lines. Clever built-ins gave the house a craftsman feel. It was decorated in what Sadie called Wyoming ranch chic, with cow hide rugs and leather couches mingling with portraits of wildlife and natural river rock on the enormous living room fireplace. Claire and Sadie moved through the house quickly, murmuring to each other.

"This room would be perfect for the twins," Sadie joked.

"I was thinking we could move your parents into this one," Claire replied, musing.

"I think Kendall would like the view out of this window."

Claire peered out the window Sadie gestured at, then frowned at the porch roof outside the window. "Yes, but she'd be able to sneak out too easily. Can't watch that one too closely." Sadie snickered.

"There's room for your roller skates in this closet."

"There's room for the whole team's roller skates in this closet," Claire whistled, her voice echoing in the main bedroom's gigantic dressing room.

"Hey, check this out," Sadie said, and Claire came to look over her shoulder at the built-in dresser drawers. Men's clothes were stacked neatly inside. Sadie opened one of the closet doors and saw a line of freshly ironed button up shirts and pressed jeans hanging above a row of fancy cowboy boots. Several hatboxes with STETSON emblazoned on them filled the top shelf.

Claire sniffed and then coughed. "It smells like cologne," she whispered.

"Is this Preston's stuff? Is he living in this model home?" Sadie closed the closet and entered the attached bathroom, an echoey, floor-to-ceiling marble monstrosity with an infinity soaking tub overlooking the mountain view. She opened a few drawers before finding one that held a leather dopp kit. The same cologne scent wafted up, and she blanched. It was strong and smelled like tobacco and leather. "I think so?" she hissed at Claire, gesturing at the dopp kit.

She pulled a face. "That's not the behavior of someone that's doing okay with money," she mused.

"Unless he's just cheap?"

Claire shook her head. "He inherited a lot of money, Sadie. Enough that he doesn't have to act cheap."

They puzzled over that as they toured the rest of the house.

In no time at all, they were back on the ground floor and entering Erica's office to take seats in front of her desk.

"Can I answer questions about the house?"

"It's not the floor plan we would choose," Claire said. "And I hate that main bathroom. So much cold marble." She reached for the packet on the table and flipped it open, scanning through the floor plan options. "Ooh, Sadie, I like this one."

Sadie looked at it. The starting cost was listed as $7.5 million. Of course Claire would like that one best.

"Mmm," Sadie said noncommittally. She needed to figure out how to ask about the water. "Is there an option for a pool?"

Erica smiled. "There is. It's one of the last pages of the brochure. There's actually an abundance of local hot springs nearby, including the one you drove by on your way here. Astoria? Many residents choose to use those pools instead. We have an agreement with them to offer private soak times for residents, including a key to get in after hours. But if you'd like a pool of your own, we have engineering plans on how to pipe into the hot springs for your own natural warm pool."

"Wow," Claire said, her eyes widening as she looked over those plans. It must have cost a veritable fortune for billionaire Claire to think it was expensive.

"Are the houses on wells, then?" Sadie asked. She hoped her question seemed seamless.

"No," Erica said, shaking her head and making her curls bob. "The initial lots drilled wells, but Mr. Chandler decided it would be better for the housing development to be on a central water system. All water is put through a seven stage reverse osmosis filtration process, and it's optional to add a whole-home filter on your house as well."

Sadie frowned. "Why would the ground quality not be good enough?"

Erica didn't blink. "It's of okay quality, but residents of Chandler Estates expect more than that."

"Oh." Sadie was at a loss.

Claire cleared her throat. "Now, Sadie-boo, I know you like to have all the information before we make a decision, but I'm sure it's fine."

Erica's eyes glinted. "Are you interested, then?"

Claire shrugged. "We need a place. This could work for now, don't you think?"

Sadie forced herself to pretend she had enough money to buy a $7.5 million dollar house to get them through until they could find something else she liked. "But the time, too, shmoopie," she said, batting her eyes at Claire.

"Current build times are about nine months, if financing isn't required..." Erica said, looking at them expectantly.

"Financing?" Claire said it like she'd never heard the word before. "Oh, that's not a consideration."

"We'll need to discuss it more," Sadie said firmly. Claire sighed, but closed the brochure. "What else do you need to know?"

"The water thing is still eating at me. Do you have any water quality tests from the source, pre-treatment, I can see the data for?"

"My Sadie's a scientist," Claire said, fluttering her eyelashes at Sadie and putting her hand on her knee. "She likes to have all the information before deciding. I like to just jump in, you know? But it's her money, after all."

Sadie suppressed a grin. She was a rich scientist? That seemed less believable than that they'd met at a roller derby match and were from Chicago.

"Of course. We can provide you with the test information," Erica said, standing and going to a filing cabinet. She pulled out a folder, then pulled out a stapled packet and handed it to Sadie. "Here's the last three years of water quality samples taken from our filtration facility. You can take those with you. If you have questions, the name of our environmental coordinator is included on the back page."

That certainly was upfront of them. Maybe this was a dead end after all. Sadie didn't look at the pages. "Thank you," she said to Erica sincerely.

Claire stood. "We'll be in touch."

Sadie stood as well. "Oh yes, we will. We need to be off, anyway. We have a dogsled tour scheduled."

"Oh, how fun. Up to Pritchard Hot Springs? I wasn't sure it was open after–" she broke off and averted her eyes.

Sadie eyed Erica. "After what?"

Erica cleared her throat. "Oh, some nasty business with a local up there. Definitely call the Forest Service to check and see if they're open before going up there."

"Our tour is to Granite Hot Springs, actually," Sadie said.

"Oh, how nice," Erica smiled.

Claire hustled Sadie out before she could make up any more stories. In the back of the SUV, hurtling back towards Hoback Junction, Sadie opened the packet of information. Her stomach dropped. There, on the three-year trend graph, was the same suspect wave she'd seen in the packet from Poplar.

# Chapter Twenty-Four

Francesca was in working order again, though she'd always carry the battle scars of the vandalism. They were waiting for a supply order, but other than that, the coffee kiosk was almost back in business. Since it was already midday Friday and the promised snowstorm was bearing down on them, Sadie decided to stay closed Saturday and reopen officially on Monday. She closed up the kiosk after texting the plan to Kendall, then climbed into her Subaru and turned on the engine for it to warm up.

The packet of paperwork from Preston Chandler's development caught her eye, and she heaved a sigh. She was out of her depth. The homeowners at Chandler Estates wouldn't take the news that the water they'd been told was filtered seven times before being pumped into their houses was contaminated with nitrates, and possibly not fit for human consumption. The data being identical was too much for Sadie. Surely that meant that the Chandler Estates tests were faked, too?

Meadow had connected Royce and Preston. Royce had been faking water tests. The water tests for Preston's real estate development showed the same fake repeating variation as the Poplar tests. The connection seemed clear. But if Preston was living there, wouldn't he care about the faked water tests? He was using the water too. And why was he living there? Why was he in such a money crunch if he'd inherited so much? Why had he changed the water system from individual wells to a group system with a filtration plant servicing everyone?

Sadie needed to take this information to the police. It was the right thing to do, even if she'd rather avoid Detective Nolan. A car moving by on the highway caught her eye, and she looked up in time to see an unmarked black SUV following a Jackson Hole Police Department sedan and several other law enforcement vehicles down the highway towards Poplar. Hmm. Speak of the police themselves.

Curious, Sadie put on her seatbelt and pulled away from the kiosk. If they were headed to Poplar, she wanted to know what they were up to. Plus, she could talk to the detective about what she'd found at Chandler Estates.

* * *

Sadie ended up a few cars behind the law enforcement convoy, so by the time she pulled into Poplar, the action was already happening. Police cars had surrounded Jerry Givens' trailer home, and Officer Knott was leading Jerry down the steps of his porch with his arms cuffed behind him.

Sadie pulled into the driveway at Jake's house and got out to gape. *Jerry? Really? It was too obvious. Plus, he had an alibi!* Sadie wondered again what they might have found in his house when they executed the search warrant. They had to have had probable cause to do so, which means they must have found something somewhere. They couldn't get a warrant just because Jerry and Royce had fought the day he died, right?

Someone was beside Sadie then, and she turned abruptly to see Jake standing there.

"Looks like they got him, huh?"

Sadie grumbled. "I dunno. It doesn't fit for me. Jerry had an alibi. And he hasn't hid that he disliked Royce at all."

Jake made a noise that led Sadie to believe he agreed with her.

"Plus, I found additional evidence that makes me think it might have been Preston Chandler after all."

"Really? What?"

Sadie quickly filled Jake in on her and Claire's sleuthing and the doctored water tests.

"You've got to tell the detective!"

Sadie nodded. "I know. I was deciding to do that when I saw him drive down, that's why I'm here." Jerry was in the back of a police car now. She could see Detective Nolan standing, talking to another officer. "Do you think I should go over there now? Or, maybe I should just call him."

"I don't know that I'd approach. Maybe call?"

Sadie agreed. She ducked back into her Subaru to dig through her purse and find the business card the detective had given her. She dialed the number on her cell and watched the detective. He felt or heard his phone go off, looked down at the caller ID, and immediately looked at her across the circle. Sadie gave a half wave.

"Yes, Ms. Moose?" He sounded brusque as he answered.

"I need to talk to you about some evidence I found."

"We're pretty busy at the moment, as I'm sure you can tell."

"*You* don't look that busy," Sadie chided. "Come over here when you're done? You'll want to see this."

Sadie could see his jaw clench from across the circle. He didn't seem like he was in a good mood.

"I'll be over soon," he snapped, and hung up.

Jake pulled Sadie inside after that. He made her a cup of tea while she sat at his kitchen table, thinking.

"Does Jerry have a snowmobile?"

"Yes. I think the only people here that don't are me, the roommates, and Meadow. But everyone has access to the one parked behind the shop for emergencies. We all know where the key is."

"Oh!" Sadie said suddenly. "That reminds me. The roommates, or actually, I think they're a throuple, they wanted me to ask you if you'd co-sign their application for additional housing."

Jake frowned. "I don't think I've been here long enough for my signature to count for anything."

Sadie shrugged. "Maybe not, but they asked nicely. And really, it's pretty shitty that Royce wouldn't help them because they're not the kind of family he wanted here."

Jake's jaw clenched. "That's true. Sure, I'll do it. I'll go talk to them later."

Sadie winced. "Maybe just text them."

Jake raised an eyebrow at her.

"Gen Z, man. They hate talking to people."

"Okay, fine, I'll email them."

"Anyway, what kind of event would warrant an emergency snowmobile?" Sadie asked.

"Blizzard. Getting snowed in. Needing to go out for medicine or supplies. The Wi-Fi at the top of the mountain going out in the middle of winter and needing to be repaired."

"Doesn't that happen all the time?"

"Yep. We use the emergency snowmobile a lot for that."

Jake stood up straight and whipped around to look at her.

"Shit."

"What?"

"I never thought about that. The trail to get to the Wi-Fi equipment goes up the backside of the mountain the hot springs are on. It's simple enough to go up that way, then go down and around the mountain."

Sadie stared at him.

"So you're saying someone could've come back a different way after murdering Royce?"

Jake looked grim. "Yes. I can't believe I never thought of it before now."

"Who all knows about the back way? Surely Elaina knows."

Jake shook his head. "Elaina's never been up to fix the Wi-Fi, at least as far as I know. I went up with Royce in December, so I'd know how to do it while he was on an ice fishing trip. Me, Carl, Darnell, Cole, and Justin are the only ones that have been up there besides Royce."

The kettle whistled and Jake turned to take it off the burner and poured a stream of water into a heavy pottery mug for Sadie. He handed her the mug, and she plopped her chosen herbal tea bag into it. Jake poured his own cup and sat at the table with her.

They sat in silence as they blew on their tea and sipped. The only sounds were the wood crackling in the fireplace and the clicking of the stove as it cooled down. The sound of Sadie's phone dinging a text notification startled her enough that she sloshed her tea out of the cup, cursing as she did so.

Jake got up to get her a cool washcloth to ease the burn as she clicked open the notification. It was a text from her multi-level-marketing-slinging college friend, Amy. Sadie sighed. It was probably a request for her to host an online party, or a notification that she was running a flash sale. Sadie liked to support her friends in their businesses—she herself was a business-woman after all—but she didn't like the way the company Amy represented ran things. It felt scammy and predatory, and she worried about how much Amy had sunk into it. Bracing herself for a sales pitch, she swiped open the message.

Hey, friend! My upline is looking for a
house to rent in Jackson Hole for a retreat in
April. Do you know anything about this one? It
looks remote, but how cool to have hot springs
nearby!

Oh. So not a sales pitch. Sadie clicked the link. Her internet browser loaded a simple webpage advertising the Pritchard Hot Springs Retreat. As the pictures loaded, Sadie's heart beat faster.

"What is it?" Jake asked. Sadie glanced up at him, realizing he'd said her name several times. He was holding out the cool washcloth for her hand. Sadie took it and handed him her phone.

"Uh...isn't this advertising that private inholding up the road from the hot springs as a private retreat?"

Jake scrolled through the ad, a furrow appearing between his brows.

"It looks like it, yeah. That must be new."

"I thought Cole took care of it since it was empty?"

"I...thought that too. Look, here's two numbers to call to reserve it." Jake grabbed his own phone and paged through his contacts. He stared down at his phone, then the number on the webpage, then his phone again, finally putting both phones down on the table before looking back up at her, his expression strained.

"It's Cole's number. And...Amos's."

# Chapter Twenty-Five

A knock at the door shocked them both from where they sat, staring at one another. Sadie's mind was whirling. It was not a great time to talk to the detective. For a minute, Sadie considered ducking under the table to hide until she was ready to talk to him, but then she remembered he could see her through the open shade on the front door and she abandoned that half-baked plan.

Sadie looked at Jake and reached over to turn off the screen of her phone. They didn't know that this new information was connected to Royce's murder at all. They didn't need to mention it. Jake shut his phone screen off too and gave her a nod. He got it. They'd leave Amos and Cole out of this until they had a better idea what was going on. He got up to let the detective in, offering a cup of tea.

The room felt suddenly small with both men in it. Detective Nolan stomped the snow off his boots and then made his way over to the table to sit next to Sadie. Jake poured a mug of steaming water and pushed it and the basket of tea options over towards him as he sat down. Sadie watched as he selected an English Breakfast and dunked the tea bag in.

"So, Jerry, huh?"

Detective Nolan raised an eyebrow at her. "You know I can't talk about it."

"For the murder? And the vandalism of my coffee kiosk? And the house fire?"

"Good questions, Sadie," Jake said. "It's about time you got an update on the vandalism."

The detective looked between them and finally lifted his shoulders in defeat. "Okay. You got me. Yes. For the murder of Royce and for the vandalism. The house fire, we're not sure about yet. It's not completely clear it was intentional."

"I thought Jerry had an alibi."

"His cousin isn't a reliable source, and no one else can verify it. Jerry has access to a snowmobile. His whereabouts cannot be confirmed for the time in question. He knew the route to the hot springs. He could have snuck up on Royce and hit him over the head, resulting in him falling into the hot springs unconscious and drowning. He had the motive to do so. He was angry at Royce, and had attacked him earlier in the day and showed no remorse for it even after being charged with assault. He's a forester, and we found powder blue spray paint in his truck. He doesn't have an alibi for the night your coffee kiosk was vandalized." He paused, shrugged. "Tell me how it isn't Jerry."

"You don't have any physical evidence?"

"Cases can be made without it, you know. Not everything is like CSI. But, I didn't say we didn't have any physical evidence."

"We didn't see Jerry come back down from the hot springs."

"He could've hidden up the road when he heard you coming." *Or taken another route,* Sadie thought, but she didn't offer that information. Not yet, at least.

"When would they have decided to meet up? Do you have a record of them talking to one another?"

"We don't, but Royce's records don't show him making plans to meet up with anyone. Jerry could've seen Royce going that way and followed him up."

Sadie looked at Jake. He nodded his head towards the packet. She took a deep breath.

"Well, I don't think it was Jerry. I think it was Preston Chandler."

The detective squinted at her. "Who now?"

Sadie suppressed a sigh. Really. What kind of investigator hadn't heard about Preston Chandler? Hadn't Meadow told him about him? "He's the developer of the multi-million dollar homes across the red bridge, Chandler Estates? Meadow saw him arguing with Royce the day of Royce's murder."

A look of recognition lit up the detective's hawkish face. "Right. I wasn't able to put a name to the description she gave me. You know it was Preston Chandler?"

"I'm reasonably certain. I went by the housing development today and asked some questions of the realtor working in their model home, and she gave me the past three years of test results from their water quality tests when I asked."

The detective's eyebrows rose. "How nice of her."

Sadie shrugged. "A sleuth has her ways." She opened the packet to the page with the trend graph and pushed it over to him. Jake reached behind him to the counter to pull the packet of papers from the Ranger and laid them next to the other packet.

The detective's eyes narrowed. "Tell me what I'm looking at."

Sadie explained the trend lines shouldn't be that same repeating variation repeatedly, that it was a statistical impossibility. That the results were the same, and they knew one set had been faked, so the other set was faked, too. She told him that Royce had been spending a lot of money lately, and had been sending checks to Lauren and his son without explaining where the money came from. And her suspicion that Preston was running short on cash and staying in the model home.

When she was done, she sat back and took a sip of tea.

"So what's your theory then, Sadie?" The detective's piercing blue eyes bored into her. "Tell me how Preston Chandler had the motive, means, and opportunity to kill Royce, vandalize your coffee kiosk, and possibly burn down Royce's house."

Sadie gulped. "Well…Meadow said she overheard Royce tell Preston he would talk to him later, leading me to believe that's who Royce planned to meet at the hot springs. They made those plans orally, so they wouldn't need to text one another or whatever. I think Royce had been faking the water tests to protect Preston's housing development, and Preston had been paying Royce. Maybe Royce decided he wasn't going to fake it anymore, finally having a crisis of conscience, and Preston killed him to keep it quiet because he was out of money to pay him more."

"How did he get to the hot springs and back down again?"

"A snowmobile?"

"Do you know if Preston Chandler can ride a snowmobile? If he owns one?"

Sadie bit her lip. "No…"

"Can you see Preston Chandler obtaining specialized tree paint,"—score one for Jake, he'd been right after all—"then going to your kiosk in the middle of the night and using it to cover the cameras and then bashing in your windows and door?"

"And stealing the cinnamon moose."

"And stealing the cinnamon moose," Detective Nolan said. His voice was amused.

"Well…no, honestly. But I'm sure Preston has people that do things like that for him. And I only met him once, for a couple minutes, before I ever thought he was a suspect. I'm sure you, as a detective, would have a better impression of him than I would."

"And why would Preston kill Royce without having a backup plan in place? Surely he knew when the tests were done. Why didn't he try to bribe the forest engineer that would do them instead of Royce? Or try some other subterfuge to postpone the tests?"

Yikes. That was a good question, and Sadie didn't know. Darn.

"That would be a good question to ask Preston?"

"Right. I will talk to him. These test results are suspect, and need to be investigated. Probably not by me, because I don't think it's related to my case against Jerry, who I believe killed Royce, but by someone. I'll ensure it's followed up on. In the meantime..." he stood, papers in hand, his voice trailing off. "Please don't accuse anyone else of any crimes without running your theories by me first. Thanks for the tea." And with that, he left.

There was silence for a long moment as they listened to his boots pound down the porch steps. The wood stove crackled.

"What a dick," Jake said finally.

Sadie failed to suppress a laugh.

"Really. He's just jealous he didn't have the information you did."

"He's right, though."

Jake shrugged. "There are still more questions than answers. If he goes to question Preston Chandler and finds out he committed a crime, it will be because you pointed him that direction."

"A crime. You don't think he's our murderer?"

Jake thought about it for a minute, taking a sip of tea and clicking his blunt fingernails against the pottery as he did so.

"No. I agree that someone with as much to lose as Preston Chandler would have a backup plan in place before he killed Royce. Even if he's short on cash and couldn't have offered Royce more money instead of killing him, or bribed someone else, he would've covered his bases first. Killing Royce before that backup plan was in place was too dangerous."

"I think you're right."

"I still don't think it was Jerry, though."

Sadie nodded, then braced herself to talk about the Cole-shaped elephant in the room. "When I talked to Amos, he said he didn't know Cole. That website makes me think otherwise."

Jake grimaced. "Right. We need to ask Cole about that. Should I call him and ask him to come over?"

"Let me bake something first. If we're going to confront your friend and coworker about a possible scam they're running and the connection it might have to a murder, we should have baked goods to gnaw on while we do it."

* * *

While Sadie baked a batch of chocolate chip cookies, she took a screenshot of Amos and Cole's phone numbers side by side on the website and sent it in a text to Amos.

**Explain.**

Her text was brief, but she thought shifty Amos would respond best to authority. The three dots that showed her he was typing showed up immediately. Sadie punched the call button instead of waiting.

"Hello?" Amos sounded wary.

"Amos. You lied to me about not knowing Cole Richards. Tell me the truth."

"Shit. Give me a minute." She heard Lilith in the background asking who he was talking to and imagined him ducking into his guest bedroom and hiding under his Pikachu comforter. After a moment, he came back on the line.

"I–I didn't want to lie. I didn't mean to. But I knew if I told you I knew him, I'd have to explain everything."

"You were right. Explain everything. I'm going to ask Cole in about ten minutes, so think carefully about what you say."

There was silence, then a hitch of breath, and Amos spilled out the entire story. The billionaire that owned the private inholding had five homes. They rarely spent any time at the hot springs retreat. Cole had started looking after the house last winter. He'd had some buddies coming into town, and they needed a place to stay, so he let them stay there for the weekend. After that weekend, he realized he could do that and make some money on the side. This winter, he had brought Amos in on it. Amos kept the key and checked the guests in. Cole did the booking, the cleaning, and the prepping of the house for guests. Amos got a thirty percent cut of the profits to keep his mouth shut and help with the key.

"Is that it?" Sadie asked when Amos finally finished his tale.

"Yes," he said miserably.

"Was there anyone staying there the night Royce was murdered?"

"No. A party checked out Friday morning, and then there wasn't anyone booked up there until Sunday, and that party was going to stay all week. Cole had to cancel them."

"Did Royce know about this?"

"No. Absolutely not. He would've turned us in. Or wanted a cut of the money himself to stay quiet. He was a bastard. Excuse me for saying so."

"And you told me the truth about everything else? You're sure of it?"

"Yes, I swear to you, I didn't lie about anything else."

"What was in your test results that came back?"

"...Carfentanil. It's a tranquilizer."

Sadie paused.

"I didn't take it, I swear. I've never done any of the hard drugs. Pot, sure. But none of the hard stuff! I don't even know where I'd get something like Carfentanil."

Sadie's mind absorbed that new piece of information. So someone had injected Amos with a tranquilizer? How would that even have worked? How did one get ahold of that kind of anesthetic? Who in Poplar would have access to it?

"Okay, Amos. I believe you. Now don't you dare call or text Cole to get your stories straight, because Jake is walking over to get him right now to come talk to me. Swear?"

"I swear, Sadie."

They hung up, and Sadie pulled the cookies out of the oven as the timer went off. Jake left out the back door to get Cole, and she transferred the cookies onto a cooling rack. Hopefully, they'd be sweet enough Jake would be able to confront his friend, and they could understand what was going on.

# Chapter Twenty-Six

Cole came in with a smile, but as soon as he saw Sadie sitting at the table, a pile of still warm chocolate chip cookies in front of her, his face fell.

"Have you been avoiding me, Cole Richards?" She asked.

He turned to give Jake a look, but Jake's face was stern as he shut the door behind him.

"What is this, man?" Cole protested.

"You need to answer some questions," Jake said cooly. "Take a seat."

Frustration rolled off of Cole's shoulders as he stomped across the floor, but he took the seat next to the window and crossed his arms over his chest. Jake followed him, joining them at the table.

"You sure are defensive for someone with nothing to tell me," Sadie said.

Cole let out a snort. "You're not any type of authority."

"Hey!" Jake said, his voice raising. "Sadie deserves your respect. Stop acting like a tool, man."

Cole's jaw ticked under his beard. Sadie studied him. He

really was a handsome man, but she could see the tension in his face. He swallowed hard. "I apologize for the attitude."

"Thank you," Sadie said. "Now, you and Amos Garner have been running a side hustle to rent the private inholding up above the hot springs."

Cole didn't blink.

"I don't care, particularly, about that. I feel like advertising it on the web will get you both caught eventually. While I'm all for subverting billionaires, I do know they don't take being stolen from lightly. I worry what will happen to you two when you're eventually found out."

Cole continued to stay silent.

"What I do care about, besides what will happen to the two of you, is if Royce knew about your scheme, and what he did about it."

Cole was stonily silent still.

"C'mon man," Jake said, his voice pleading. He took a chocolate chip cookie and shoved the plate closer to Cole. "Just tell the truth. I've got your back no matter what, just like in the summer, out on the line."

"I didn't kill him!" Cole burst out.

"Okay," Sadie said. "So tell me the rest."

Cole picked up a cookie and crammed the whole thing in his mouth. He closed his eyes as he chewed. Finally, when the whole cookie had been consumed, he cleared his throat and spoke.

"The guy that owns that house has been here one time in three years. It's a beautiful house, in a beautiful place, that's never, ever used. It's sad. I'm grateful for the extra cash for taking care of it, but last spring before the road closed during the thaw, I had a group of college buddies in town whose Airbnb fell through last minute. I put them up there, and they loved it, and that's when I realized I could rent it out so people get to enjoy it."

"And you make some cash."

Cole sighed. "Yes. I make some cash. But you know what it's like here." He looked at them both earnestly. "Everything costs a fortune. Holly hasn't been working, and we had bills to pay from Violet's birth. She was in the NICU for a few weeks, and even with insurance, that doesn't come cheap. We rely on summer overtime to pay the winter bills, and last year was a slow fire season."

Jake nodded. "I know that man."

"I knew it was wrong, but it didn't feel like an actual crime. If anything had happened to the house while someone was staying in it, I would've taken care of it. But nothing ever did. I screened people closely, and had strict rules and a high cleaning deposit, and Amos or I checked on them regularly. Everyone was respectful. It seemed like a win-win."

"Did you bring Amos in on purpose, or did he catch you?"

"I brought it up to him, and he was in from the start. The contractor doesn't pay him much up there. And he's a bored kid, trying to do the right thing. This gave him a little excitement at least."

"Okay. Now address the last part. I have a witness that says they saw you and Royce back behind the wood pile having words two weeks ago. Did Royce find you out?"

Cole ran his hand over his beard and let out a breath. "Of course he did. That asshole couldn't keep his nose out of anyone's business. He turned in Jerry and DeeDee for running side businesses. He hassled Meadow about not clearing her snow regularly, since she's out of town with her boyfriend all the time. He refused to support Sydney, Travis, and Megan in their housing petition because he didn't approve of their relationship. He did everything he could to avoid helping Darnell and Tamia because, on top of everything, he was racist, too. He gouged Jake on firewood. I'm sure every person on this compound had a grudge against him."

Sadie thought about that. So that's why Meadow and Royce had been seen having words. And the three roommates were actually a throuple, like she'd wondered at the house party. And Darnell's suspicions were true, too. Royce hadn't been a nice man. But he was dead. Who had killed him?

"What did he threaten you with?"

Cole let out a short bark of a laugh. "He threatened to turn me in if I didn't give him a cut of the profits. He didn't care about right and wrong, he only cared about getting a piece of the action."

"And what did you tell him?"

"That he could go fuck himself...and then about a week later I agreed to cut him in, but I'd decided to stop doing it at the end of the season. I'd pushed my luck far enough."

Sadie thought that through. "What did you see that night, up at the hot springs?"

"I saw nothing, I swear. I went up to clean the house after the guests had checked out. I talked to Amos on the way up, but there were still people in the hot springs then. When I left the house, I came straight home and didn't turn into the hot springs at all."

"Have you been up to the house since? Could someone have hidden out there?"

Cole glanced out the window and then sighed. "Yes. I went up the back way on Saturday to check things out. I didn't see any new tracks headed to the house. I don't think anyone hid up there."

"You went the back way?" Jake asked.

"Yeah."

"On Saturday. After the snow had covered everything?"

"Yeah, I was the only tracks up there."

"Dang."

"Why?"

"If it was someone from Poplar, they probably came back that way instead of down the main road, don't you think?"

Cole blinked at him. "But the only people that know that route are you, me, Darnell, Carl, and Justin."

Jake nodded uneasily. "I know."

"If it wasn't me, and it wasn't you, you're saying it was Darnell, Carl, or Justin?"

"Darnell and Tamia were at the movies," Sadie said.

"So it was Carl or Justin?" Cole said, his voice incredulous.

Sadie shrugged. "If that's the criteria we're using, then yes, we'd narrow it down to them. Maybe Justin was angry at Royce for threatening DeeDee's business?"

Cole barked out a laugh. "Justin would be thrilled if DeeDee had to close her 'business'. It's cost them a fortune in makeup she can't sell. It's a classic pyramid scheme."

They were all silent for a moment.

"But what would Carl's motive be? I don't get it."

"Does he have an alibi?"

Sadie considered. "He told me he was home all night, and that DeeDee could confirm his truck never left the driveway."

"But his snowmobile?"

"Good question."

They were interrupted by Sadie's phone ringing. She glanced down at the display, which said Paige. Paige never called, preferring to text. Sadie frowned as she answered. "Hello?"

"Sadie! I think something's wrong, and I can't get ahold of Mateo. Can you come to the hospital with me?"

Sadie's heart raced. "I'm down in Poplar, but I'll leave right this second, babe. Are you okay?"

Paige was crying. "I'm not sure."

"Okay. Do you want to go to the hospital and I'll meet you?"

"No, I want you to come get me."

Sadie was standing, shoving her feet into boots and grabbing her coat and purse. Jake looked concerned.

"I'll be there as fast as I can," Sadie promised. "It's Paige," Sadie hissed at Jake. "I'm going to town."

"Do you want me to drive you?" Jake opened the door for her as she bustled out.

"I'm hanging up now, Paige, so I can drive. If you feel worse, call 911 or get to the hospital immediately!"

"I will," Paige promised, and she hung up.

"No, it's okay," Sadie answered Jake. "I'm just going to go straight to her house and get her. She says she thinks something's wrong with the baby."

Cole was standing behind Jake. "Then you better get going. We'll keep thinking about what's going on here. Go take care of your friend."

Sadie gave a half smile to Cole. "I will." She kissed Jake on the cheek, then turned to rush down the steps to her car, her heart in her throat. Paige and Mateo had tried for a baby for so long. Nothing bad could happen to them. As she pulled out onto the icy highway, she repeated that mantra repeatedly. *Nothing bad was going to happen. Nothing bad was going to happen. Nothing bad was going to happen.*

# Chapter Twenty-Seven

"Your baby and you are both fine."

Paige let out a sob, and Sadie wrapped an arm around her shoulders as she took a deep breath. It had been a tense few hours, first driving into town white-knuckled, then picking up a crying Paige and driving her to the hospital. Paige hadn't wanted to talk about what was going on, but eventually, Sadie figured out she was bleeding and cramping. She'd been checked into a room in the emergency department. A nurse hooked her up to a fetal monitor while they went to get an ultrasound machine and her midwife was called. Sadie had held Paige's hand while she lay still, monitoring band around her belly sending a jagged line of data to the machine neither of them could interpret. When the midwife had finally come in with the nurse and ultrasound machine, they'd both been quivering, crying messes.

But one look on the ultrasound monitor, and they'd both let out sighs of relief. They could see the little profile of baby Gates-Ortiz, little fists pumping, legs kicking. Despite Paige's worrying symptoms, the baby didn't seem in distress. After an exam, the midwife confirmed their hopes.

"I see a small subchorionic hematoma on the placenta, and that's what causing the bleeding. The placement isn't particularly worrisome, and baby is happy. I'm going to admit you overnight for further monitoring, but I think you'll be able to go home and resume normal activity with weekly monitoring tomorrow."

It was then Mateo finally burst into the room, and after squeezing Paige's hand, Sadie stepped outside to make room for him. She could hear him apologizing profusely, rapidly explaining that he'd been meeting with a client at his construction site up Fall Creek Road and hadn't had cell service. Sadie heard Paige murmuring back to him, and the dulcet tones of the midwife's calming voice explaining everything again, and smiled. She loved that family so much, and she couldn't wait to snuggle that baby, but she could wait until June when they were due.

She made her way down the hall towards the waiting room, figuring she'd give them all some time before she told them goodbye, and turned the corner only to run straight into someone.

"Oh," Sadie exclaimed, "I'm so sorry!" She stepped back, grabbing onto the wall to steady herself, then looked up at who she'd run into. It was Carl Brent.

"Are you okay, Sadie?" He asked, his voice calm.

"Yes, I'm so sorry. Again, I didn't see you there."

He nodded at her. He was standing outside a door labeled "LAB", a packet of papers in his hands. Sadie's interest was piqued, but she didn't want to be overly nosy. Her gut was reminding her that just a couple of hours ago, she'd been theorizing that he could've killed Royce. In his calm presence now, though, in the glaring fluorescent lights of a hospital hall, she had a hard time seeing how this stoop-shouldered, graying man with a sad face could be a murderer.

"Are you okay?" She asked him. He blinked at her. "I mean, I didn't hurt you when I ran into you, did I?"

"No, I'm fine." He paused. "I'm just getting my testing done that the Ranger set up."

"Oh, right. Jake has his scheduled for next week."

"That's good. Are you doing it as well?"

Sadie thought about it. "I've only used the water down there a few times. I don't think I will."

Carl's face twisted. "I would get it done, anyway. You can't be too safe."

Sadie thought again about Carl's late wife, wondering if the water quality issues could have been an influence on her cancer.

"Thanks for the advice, Carl. I'll consider it."

Sadie stepped around him, but he stopped her with a gentle hand on her arm and she looked up at him.

"Have you...found out anything else about Royce's murder?"

Sadie was surprised by the question. Surprised enough, she answered him without thinking. "I've found out a few things. Speaking of the water quality, though, I found out that the water tests at Chandler Estates show the same data inconsistencies as the ones at Poplar."

Carl's face drained of color. His grip on her arm tightened.

"Preston Chandler?" He said, his voice brittle. He was standing close, his intense face close to hers. Sadie smelled cinnamon, and it made her think of something, but the pain of his grasp wouldn't let her shake the thought loose.

"Carl, you're hurting my arm," Sadie said, her voice a little louder than she'd meant. He released it then, looking away from her. "And yes, Preston Chandler. Do you know him?"

"I've seen him around. So he was the one that put Royce up to it, then? To save his fancy development?"

"I'm not sure of that, but it's a theory. Hey—are you okay?" Sadie looked around. Carl didn't look well. His complexion had gone pale, but his cheeks were reddening. His breaths were coming in shorter gasps. She saw his jaw tense. "Do you need a doctor?"

"No," he bit out. "I'm fine, Sadie. I have to go."

And with that, he stalked away, his booted feet stomping on the linoleum floors towards the exit.

"Make someone else mad, Sadie Moose?"

Sadie turned toward the new voice, smiling as she recognized Hector, her favorite nurse who had cared for her last fall when she'd spent almost a week in the hospital after a concussion.

"Oh, you know," Sadie said, "I make friends everywhere I go."

"You do when you bring baked goods," Hector said, deadpan.

"Is that a not-so-subtle hint I need to send in a box?"

"It'll go a long way the next time you're in here busted up."

Sadie shuddered. "I hope that's not soon, but I could use all the credit I could get. Actually, Hector, I had a question for you. What can you tell me about the tranquilizer Carfentanil?"

Hector blinked at her. "I don't know that one. Come with me to the nurse's station and I'll look it up."

Sadie fell into step with him. "Nice scrubs, by the way." The scrub top was patterned with Garfield stating that he hated Mondays.

Hector did a shimmy. "You always liked Garfield the best."

At the nurse's station, Hector plopped into a chair and logged into a computer, taking a swig from the iced coffee he'd left at the station. He pulled up a reference website, then typed in the name after Sadie told it to him again.

"Hmmm..." he said. "Well, there's your problem, Moose. You're at the wrong place. You want a veterinary clinic."

* * *

Sadie walked to her car without even realizing it, coming back to herself once she was inside with the motor running, the car heating. She hadn't even said goodbye to Paige and Mateo.

But her brain was whirling with the new information from Hector that Carfentanil was a veterinary tranquilizer. What was it? What had she forgotten? Sadie was overwhelmed with the feeling that she had all the pieces she needed to solve this puzzle now. If only she could figure out how they went together. Her fingers itched for a pad of paper to make a list, and she opened her purse to dig around for a notepad and a pen. She pawed past a rolled up newspaper, and she suddenly remembered.

*Shit.*

She reached into her pocket for her phone and pulled up her browser, typing in the Jackson Hole Journal web address and waiting for it to pull up. The page refused to load, and she checked her signal, frowning to see she only had one bar of service. Connectivity could be finicky even in the town of Jackson, with the mountains all around and the tourists in town jamming the towers. She could run back into the hospital and see if she could connect to Wi-Fi. But there was another option.

She dialed a number, placed the phone on speakerphone and put it in her cupholder, buckled up, and put her car into reverse, pulling out onto Broadway, her instincts taking her back towards Poplar.

"Jackson Hole Journal, you make news and we gossip about it for money," Penny's tinny voice said through the speaker.

"Penny! I need your help."

"Well, I'm your girl, but I'm right in the middle of editing a piece at the moment—Randall! You're forty-two years old and a professional reporter. Can you learn the difference between there, their, and they're please?"

Sadie sighed, waiting for Penny's full attention while sitting at the stoplight at the town square. She'd driven past the closed bakery already. Tourists in snow gear, many in ski boots, clomped by in front of her. Darkness had fallen, and the twinkly lights that went up before Christmas and stayed on through the winter lit up the night. A light snow was falling. The promised storm had arrived.

Randall and Penny were arguing loudly through the phone.

"Penny, really, I need help."

Penny broke off arguing with Randall. "What do you need?" Her voice sounded concerned for the first time.

"Last Sunday, you ran an article on a wildlife survey in the Park. I need you to read me the caption on the front-page photo again."

"I wrote that article, Sadie," Randall's voice said, his voice tinged with importance. Sadie realized she must be on speakerphone. Good thing her problem wasn't personal.

"Oh," Sadie said, pressing the gas pedal to move through the light as it finally changed. "So you were there that day?"

"You betcha."

"Sadie, the caption says, 'Bridger-Teton National Forest wildlife biologist Carl Brent collars a large male wolf, part of the Grand Teton National Park pack, after it had been tranquilized and transported to the project site last Wednesday,'" Penny said, and Sadie's heart squeezed. Right. She'd remembered correctly.

"Did you see them tranquilize any animals, Randall?"

"Most of them were tranquilized by gunners in the helicopter, but I saw them put a few of them out further using needles."

"Do you remember what tranquilizer they used? And who was administering it?"

There was silence for a few moments.

"Answer the question, Randall," Penny said impatiently.

"I'm thinking!"

Sadie's mind was whirling.

Finally, Randall's voice came back through the speaker. "I pulled up my photos from the day. There's one where if I zoom in on the drug bottle, it says Car...fentanil?"

"Oh my God."

"...and the person who was administering it on site was Carl Brent, like in the feature photo. Why, Sadie?" Sadie could hear Randall's reporter instinct kicking in. Finally. He wasn't the best reporter in town, though he was one of the only ones.

"Give me a second to think," Sadie said. She was through town now, headed south towards Hoback Junction. She'd have cell service for just a few more minutes.

Carl Brent was a wildlife biologist for the Bridger-Teton National Forest. He participated in a wildlife project that involved tranquilizing wildlife two days before the murder. Carfentanil was a popular veterinary tranquilizer. Amos had been injected with it, doused in liquor, and incapacitated while someone killed Royce Hensley. Carl Brent didn't have a verifiable alibi. Carl Brent knew the back way to the hot springs. Carl Brent smelled like cinnamon, like the missing cinnamon moose from her coffee kiosk. Carl Brent had a motive—his wife's illness. If Carl had found out about Royce faking the water tests, would that have been enough to move him to murder?

Sadie thought about the look on Carl's face when he'd heard about Preston Chandler, and she knew, then, that it would have been enough.

And Preston Chandler was next.

She needed to warn him! But how? Paige had his card, but

she was in the hospital. She couldn't bug her unless she really needed to. She should call Detective Nolan, but she'd just accused Preston of murder a few hours ago, and he hadn't been happy about it. If she called him now to say she thought he was in danger because someone else was the murderer? He'd think she was a joke. Sadie remembered what she and Claire had found in the model home. Maybe Sadie could go by and warn him, just until she could convince the detective to question Carl.

"Sadie?"

Penny's voice was loud, and she had a feeling it wasn't the first time she'd said her name.

"Yeah," Sadie said. She squinted at the road. The snow was falling thicker. She slowed down. "Listen, Penny. Can you call Greg and tell him I'm going to the model home at Chandler Estates to talk to Preston Chandler, and I think Carl Brent is headed that way too? And that Carl was the one that murdered Royce?"

"Sadie, you're breaking up–" Penny's voice crackled through the speaker.

*Damn. I should pull over to talk to her.* But with the lack of visibility in the snow, Sadie was worried she might get hit if she pulled over, or hit someone else when she tried to pull back out. It really was falling fast.

"Call Greg!" Sadie tried again. "Tell them I'm going to Chandler Estates. Preston Chandler's house!"

"Who?"

"Preston! Chandler!" Sadie yelled.

*Beep beep beep.* Her phone dropped the call. And then it was just Sadie, on the dark highway in a blizzard, headed towards a dubious scenario, her heart pounding fast. She knew she could drive by the entrance to Chandler Estates, go down to Poplar, tell Jake what she knew, call the detective from there, but she couldn't shake the feeling that if she did, it might cost Preston his life. She remembered the look on Carl's face as he'd stalked away from her. It had been brutal, and full of rage. It was the look of a man who thought they'd gotten their revenge, but found they'd been foiled. The look of a man who would not waste any more time.

# Chapter Twenty-Eight

Sadie had to slow down to a crawl to negotiate the curves leading into Hoback Junction. The road was nearly empty, just one car having passed her in the last ten minutes, when she headed into the junction. It was after five o'clock, and the road would normally be packed with commuters, but they were all either still in Jackson waiting out the storm, or stuck somewhere behind her. When she finally saw the lights ahead, she sighed in relief. The safety of the market and her closed up coffee kiosk called her, but she kept driving. The reader board sign warned about slick conditions ahead, but the highway headed south past Poplar was still open. With grim determination, she stayed on the highway, the wiper blades on her Subaru working furiously to clear the snow as it fell.

It felt like an hour before she finally saw the red bridge, its twinkle lights barely visible in the snow, and turned off the highway to cross it. There was at least one set of tracks in the accumulation, so she followed those across, her knuckles turning white as she did at the thought of losing traction or going sideways on the narrow one-car-at-a-time bridge. When she was over it, she breathed a sigh of relief.

As she passed the commercial hot springs, her eye was drawn to the parking lot. There were two vehicles in it.

One was a new black Mercedes G-Wagon.

The other was a black lifted truck, like the one that had almost run her over.

She slammed on the brakes, remembering too late that the roads were slick with snow. The Subaru fishtailed, threatening to go off the road, but she pumped the brakes and turned into the skid, slowly steering the car back onto the road and coming to a stop.

Her breath was coming fast, and her heart was pounding. *Shit.*

Sadie grabbed her phone out of the cupholder and peered down at it. Of course, there was no service.

What should she do? Turn into the hot springs parking lot, creep around, see what was going on? Turn around, drive to Poplar, call the police? Obviously, that was the right decision. And she needed to hurry.

Sadie let her foot off the brake and hit the gas. A loud thumping sound emanated from her front tires, and her back wheels spun. The whole car shuddered with the effort.

*Oh no.*

*Oh no no no.*

She put it in reverse and tried to back up, and got nowhere.

"Fuck!" she yelled.

Forward, try it, backward try it. It was no use. She was only getting her car more and more stuck in the rapidly accumulating snow.

Sadie dropped her head to the steering wheel. Now what? She had well and truly fucked up this time. She was stuck in the middle of the road in a blizzard with a probable revengeful killer stalking his next victim just feet away.

Right. If she was stuck, the least she could do was try to help Preston Chandler. He didn't deserve the help, but no one deserved to die. And maybe if the hot springs building was open, she'd be able to find a phone, call for help, then hide before anyone saw her. Her only other options were to wait for someone else to come by, or try getting out and walking, and either could be a death sentence in this weather.

Faced with either freezing to death or trying to save a man's life, her choice was obvious.

Grimly, she dug around in her backseat for a scarf, winding it around her neck. She shoved on her coat, warmest gloves, and hat, then put her phone in her pocket. She wished desperately for a weapon, but there was nothing in her car to help her. She turned off her headlights and flipped on her emergency flashers. With a deep breath, she pushed open her door.

The snow was falling so heavily now she could barely see the hot springs building, even though she was on the road just outside the parking lot. It fell in wet, heavy flakes, and when she stepped out, the snow covered the tops of her boots. No wonder the Subaru had gotten stuck. It had all wheel drive, but low clearance. The tracks she'd followed across the red bridge were gone now, covered up. She couldn't know if they were Carl's tracks, turning into the commercial hot springs just before her, or if they were some other vehicle that had continued on. She wished she knew how long he'd been there. She'd probably left about fifteen minutes after him, but she hadn't known where she was going.

She shut the door behind her. The sound was muffled, like all sound in the heavy snow. She strained her ears to hear traffic on the highway—there was none—or sounds coming from the hot springs—there were none. With trepidation, she started the slow walk across the parking lot.

* * *

As Sadie neared the building, she thought about everything she knew about Astoria Hot Springs. Built recently as a replacement for a pool that had existed until flooding in the 1990s, nothing had been at the site until a recent effort by nostalgic townspeople brought the new pools to fruition. This modern building was a one-story cabin with glass doors at the entrance that led to the lobby, snack bar, and entrance to the pool deck. To the left of the lobby were the changing rooms, which exited out to the pool as well. The hot springs pools were inspired by nature, with large natural boulders and waterfalls lining the edges. There were multiple pools, including a zero depth entry kid pool, and hot, adult-only pools lower on the hillside closer to the Snake River. Sadie had been here one time before, for a party last summer. She tried to remember every detail of the layout as she crept towards the glass doors.

There were no lights on inside except the emergency exit lights above the doors. They were definitely closed. Because that was normal on a Friday at almost six o'clock at night in the winter, or because of the storm, Sadie wasn't sure. She hid behind a wood pillar outside and peered in. She didn't see any movement. Whoever was there wasn't in the lobby. With a held breath, she crept towards the doors and tried one. It was locked. She cursed.

Then she tried the other one, expecting it be locked, and was surprised when it opened freely in her hand. She opened it further and paused, listening for any sounds. She heard none. She slipped inside, holding the door so it wouldn't slam, and stood still again. She could hear the hum of a refrigerator in the snack bar, the clicking of a heater turning on some-where in the building. But she heard no voices, no footsteps. She looked down at the floor. There were no snowy foot-prints. She stomped hers off on the rug as quietly as she could, then steeled herself to hurry across the lobby to the reception desk.

When she got there, she peered around it, making sure no one was hiding under the desk. She bolted inside, ducking down so that no one could see her through the windows that over-looked the pool deck. The reception desk enclosed a small office with a copier, computers, and some file cabinets. Sadie knew that behind the door to her right was the snack bar. She wanted to open the door and see if anyone was in it, but she was afraid. Instead, her eyes zeroed in on the phone on the desk, and the wide screen computer monitor placed there. The screen was dark, but she bumped the mouse and drew in a quick breath when it brightened, showing a rotating view of security cameras both inside and outside the hot springs, the video blurry with snow falling. She caught a flash of movement on one and gasped.

The screen changed to another view, and she gritted her teeth. She'd almost seen something. She peered out the window at the darkened hot springs. She didn't see anyone up on the main level. Maybe the movement was down at the hot pools below?

She shook herself. She didn't need to find that out. What she needed to do was call for help.

She picked up the phone and stared at the keypad. Who should she call? 911? To report what? Her car had broken down? She was at the hot springs, and she thought something bad might happen? Based on what?

With a frown, she dialed a different number.

He picked up on the first ring.

"Sadie! Where are you? Penny just called me worried about you."

"Jake," Sadie whispered, sliding down to crouch on the floor, her eyes still on the security cameras. "I'm at Astoria Hot Springs. My car is stuck outside."

"Oh, shit, this storm is crazy, Sadie. Why are you over there?"

"Just listen, okay?"

"Okay..." He sounded nervous.

"Oh shit," she whispered, as the view on the security screen changed again, confirming her worst fears. On it, she could see a man in a stocking cap relaxing in the lowest pool, snow falling around him as he faced the snowy view of the Snake River. Behind him crept a solitary figure in a parka with something long and deadly looking in his hand.

"Sadie?"

"Ohmygod," she said, louder. They couldn't hear her all the way down there. "Carl Brent killed Royce. And he's here, at the hot springs, to confront Preston Chandler about his role in the water scandal. Shit! I think he's going to knock him over the head while he's in the pool!"

"Sadie!"

"I know! Is Elaina home? Can you go get her and tell her to bring everyone?"

"Her car's here, yeah—but you need to call the police!"

"I will. I'll call 911, but in this storm, it will take the police forever to get here. Get Elaina."

"Are you safe?"

"I'm hiding in the lobby. Shit, though, I can't let Carl kill Preston!"

"You can if it means you stay safe," Jake said. She heard a slamming door and his quick breaths and she guessed he was running to Elaina's.

"Jake, I'm going to hang up."

"No!"

"Yes, I need to call 911. And I need to watch what's happening. And figure out how to stop it."

And she hung up. She stood then, abandoning her crouch, and looked around her. She grabbed the computer mouse and clicked on the view of the pool with Carl sneaking up on Preston. It enlarged on the screen. Was there audio? She needed to hear what was going on! With a frown, she peered at the screen and wished she had her readers. She clicked a few different buttons, and suddenly audio flooded the speakers. It was just a quiet static. Carl was behind Preston on the deck now, just the pool between them. Was he going to hit him? Did he have a gun?

She scrambled for the phone to dial 911, but stopped when she heard a voice boom through the speakers.

"You."

The man in the pool jumped and turned, standing.

"What the–" he stopped. "Who the hell are you?"

"You ruined my life." Carl's voice was low and angry, and Sadie strained to hear it. She found the button to turn up the speakers and turned them all the way up. She suddenly wondered if the cameras were recording, and not sure if they were, she hurriedly started taking a video of the screen with her phone.

All the while, she was glancing around, trying to figure out how she could interrupt the scene without compromising her own safety.

"Wouldn't be the first time," Preston was saying down below, his voice amused.

"Stop it!" Carl yelled. "Don't joke with me. You killed my wife, you asshole!"

Preston was silent for a long moment. "I don't remember killing anyone's wife."

"This game you're playing," Carl said. "With the water at Poplar. She got cancer."

There was silence for a longer moment then, and Sadie's mind whirled. How long had it been since she'd called Jake? How long would it take Elaina to get here? It was a five-minute drive on a good day. In this storm, it could take a lot longer. Her eye caught on a switch on the desk and a button.

Suddenly, she had a plan. She needed to wait for the exact right moment.

"I'm sorry about that," Preston said, his voice gentle and sounding genuinely remorseful.

"I don't want your sympathy! You knew the water was bad, and you paid off fucking Royce Hensley to hide it. Why? Why did you do it?"

"It was just business. Royce was a pawn. I'm guessing you killed him? I've been wondering. You exposed my mistake."

"I killed him, alright. Told him to meet me up there so I could talk to him about his shady dealings. He had the balls to ask me which ones."

"Royce was a crook," Preston admitted.

Carl continued like Preston hadn't spoken. "I snuck up on him at the hot springs, hit him over the head, and left him to drown. It was better than he deserved."

Sadie shivered. Carl didn't mention that before killing Royce, he'd snuck up on Amos, stabbed him in the butt with a needle filled with veterinary tranquilizer, doused him in booze, and left him in his cabin. It had been a well-planned, sneakily executed, cold-blooded murder. Maybe a justified one. Sadie couldn't decide, and she thought she'd be thinking about it for the rest of her life.

"Your business caused my wife to get cancer and die! And

who knows how everyone else that lives there's health has been affected," Carl concluded.

"As far as I know, nothing as bad as cancer is possible."

"It happened to me!"

"I don't discount that," Preston said, his voice calm. The view on the camera was getting blurrier as the snow accumulated, but Sadie could see him standing calmly in the water. Was it her, or was he slightly closer to the edge where Carl stood than he had been before?

"All for your profits," Carl sneered.

"Like I said, it was business. If people knew that I'd contaminated the water with the initial well drilling, I wouldn't recoup my investment in this property. I was going to fix the Forest water system once I'd made my money back. Plus, Royce told everyone to drink bottled."

"Nitrates can effect the human body just by bathing. My wife...she only drank bottled. But she took baths. She loved her baths, throughout her illness, even. She was soaking in hot water for comfort, that you knew was still poisoning her body." Carl's voice was thick, but resolved. Preston had admitted to his part in the scheme. He'd put his need for profits above the health of dozens of people. Maybe letting Carl hit Preston over the head with whatever he held in his hand and then letting him drown was the right way to go.

But, no. The right thing to do was to have Preston Chandler publicly answer for his crimes. Carl Brent had done enough damage killing Royce. She couldn't let him kill Preston, too.

"I think that's debatable."

"Stop arguing with me!" Carl raised his arm above his head, and as if in slow motion, Preston lunged for him. It was her moment.

Sadie dropped her phone on the counter and flipped on the

floodlights while pressing the microphone button. She quickly dialed 911 on the desk phone and put it on speaker.

"911, what's your emergency?" Sadie heard through the phone, but most importantly, Carl and Preston heard down at the pool.

In a clear voice so that both the 911 dispatcher and the two men could hear her, Sadie said, "I'm at Astoria Hot Springs. There are two men here, Preston Chandler and Carl Brent. Carl Brent killed Royce Hensley, and he's threatening to kill Preston."

On the screen, Sadie watched the two men spring apart and look up towards the lobby. *Shit.* One of them was wet and lacked clothes, but the other one, the killer, was fully dressed. She should've thought this through better.

"Ma'am, authorities are en route that direction based on an earlier call." Penny! She'd gotten her message. "But with the storm, it's going to take a while," the 911 operator said, and Sadie felt her stomach drop. They'd heard that, too. She was done for. "Can you get someplace safe?"

"I'm armed," Sadie said, lying through her teeth. "And they know that I've called the police."

The 911 dispatcher paused.

On the screen, Sadie saw Carl unfreeze and turn, and she knew he was headed where she was. This was it. She released the microphone button. "I'm going to go barricade myself in the bathroom," she told the 911 dispatcher. "I've also alerted Officer Elaina Johnson, a Forest Service law enforcement officer that lives nearby, and I hope she gets here soon."

"I'll let the responding officers know. Please be safe."

Sadie hung up. She could no longer see Carl on the screen, but she could see Preston hurriedly dressing down at the water's edge. She grabbed her phone and hustled out of the reception area, turning to find a bathroom to hide in. She saw motion through the glass doors and stifled a scream, recognizing Elaina.

Elaina pushed in.

"My God, Sadie, what is going on?" She hurried over to the reception desk, looking at the monitor that showed Preston Chandler struggling into a pair of pants.

"Carl Brent killed Royce and was trying to kill Preston and he's on his way up here right now! He has some sort of weapon!"

Elaina's jaw tensed. "Run outside and get in my rig. Jake's out there. I made him swear he'd stay outside."

"I don't want to leave you!"

"Do as I say," Elaina insisted, shoving her towards the door. She clicked through the security cameras, then bolted around the desk to the glass doors that exited to the pool deck.

Reluctantly, Sadie did as Elaina said, but as she neared the exit doors, she heard Elaina yell, "get on the ground! It's over, Carl! Get on the ground now!" As she burst out the doors and straight into Jake's waiting arms, she believed her. It was over.

# Chapter Twenty-Nine

Sadie had never ridden on a snowmobile before, which felt weird as a girl from Jackson Hole, but it was true. Her family had always been more into human-powered recreation than engine-powered recreation. But snuggled up behind Jake, her arms wrapped tightly behind him, hurtling over the snow with the cold air hitting her cheeks, she felt like she could get used to this noisy, but fun, form of transportation.

They arrived at the hot springs at the back of the pack. Jake parked the snowmobile, and they both got off, took off their helmets, and joined the huddle of people that had gathered in the parking lot. They stood talking quietly for a while, then as one, they turned towards the trail towards the hot spring. They followed one another quietly, the only sounds their footsteps and the brush of snow-proof fabric as they walked. It was a dark night, the crescent moon hidden behind the clouds, so those in front had their headlamps on and others carried flashlights. They crossed the wooden bridge, recently shoveled to clear the two weeks of snow that had built up on it while the hot springs had been closed, then walked to the hot springs, opened the gate, and filed in to surround it.

Their puffs of air mingled with the steam coming off of the spring.

Elaina was again the first one to speak.

"We're here tonight to put this behind us." There were nods amongst the group. Everyone from Poplar was there. Justin and DeeDee huddled together with their three boys. Meadow had brought her boyfriend, a scruffy-looking man with dark eyes, and they stood together. Cole held Violet in her bright pink snowsuit, her head against his shoulder, Holly standing next to them. Darnell and Tamia held hands. So did Sydney, Megan, and Travis. The only one that stood apart was Jerry, who'd been released from police custody with an apology but not much else. Sadie stood next to Jake, the only outsider.

"Sadie, will you give the synopsis?" Sadie jumped when Elaina asked her. She hadn't expected that. "You were the one that put it all together," she said. "You should be the one to tell it."

Sadie glanced around, but everyone was nodding and looking at her expectantly.

Hesitantly, she took a breath, and then she started filling in the information she'd found out since that night a week ago at Astoria Hot Springs with what she'd found out before.

"Preston Chandler contaminated the water table when he drilled the initial wells and sewer system for his development. Rather than fess up and face his mistakes, he built the water treatment system. Royce did the regular water tests at Poplar, so when he got one out of normal, he put two and two together and went to Preston to extort him out of money to keep it quiet. Preston agreed, and for three years he paid Royce cash monthly to falsify the data. Preston was also paying his own environmental coordinator off. All that money added up over time, which is why he was so keen to trade the unsold lots at his development to the county for fairgrounds. He was in too deep."

Sadie paused.

"Carl started investigating what could have caused his wife's cancer in the months following her death. With the knowledge of the water troubles at Hoback Junction, he did an independent water test at his house. When the results came back out of the normal variables, he confronted Royce, who told him he'd look into it. Royce never mentioned it again, but Carl spied on him and watched him fake a water test. That's when he knew what he'd been doing. He plotted for almost a month to set Royce up, planning the date for after the next wildlife survey when he knew he could steal tranquilizers with no one noticing. He told Royce to meet him here so they could talk about it, and Royce agreed. He came up the back way so no one would see him, parked his snowmobile far enough away Amos didn't hear him, hiked to the hot springs, drugged Amos with pilfered veterinary tranquilizer, and then waited for Royce."

Everyone's eyes swiveled around the area, and Sadie could picture it in the space as she told the rest of the sordid tale. "He hid by the gate, and as soon as Royce walked through it, he hit him on the head with a piece of firewood. That knocked him out, and then he dragged him over to the pool and pushed him in, making sure he drowned. He locked the gate behind himself and left the same way he came, taking the piece of wood with him and feeding it into his wood stove when he got home."

Sadie stopped. That was the story, as Carl had told it in the back of Elaina's cruiser while they waited for the authorities as the snow fell, at least.

"And we got you involved further, risking your life," Holly said quietly. "I'm sorry, Sadie."

"I'm okay," she said. "It's okay."

"Tell the rest," Elaina said sternly.

Sadie sighed.

"Carl decided he should frame Jerry, since Jerry had conveniently fought with Royce that morning. He thought about framing Cole instead, but since Jerry lived alone, it was easier. Jerry was the one with the firewood business, and the police knew a piece of wood had been used to hit Royce. He stole tree marking paint from Jerry's shed and used it when he vandalized my coffee kiosk. He then planted the tree marking paint in Jerry's truck. He also tried to run me off the road one night. He apologized for both things, and said he hadn't meant to hurt me, just get me to stop asking questions."

"He's a slimy bastard," Jerry grumbled.

"He's a man so overcome with grief he'll blame anyone," DeeDee said quietly. "I wish I would've done more to support him in the months following Anita's death. Maybe it would've made a difference."

"You did what you could, DeeDee," Holly said. "We all tried."

They were silent again for a moment.

"He didn't start the fire, though," Sadie said, looking at Elaina, who blanched.

"Yeah, he didn't. That was his son, Dylan." Her face darkened. "That kid needs some help. I'm trying to make sure he gets it."

Sadie's heart twisted. That had been tough news to hear, but looking back at how Lauren and Dylan had acted afterwards, the story she'd seen them put together, she realized it was the truth. It sounded like Dylan was remorseful, and hadn't intended the whole house to go up, but it had happened, and Lauren had helped him cover it up, hoping their story would be believable since Royce was murdered. Sadie hoped they both got help, and the peace they both deserved.

"We had an ultrasound," Tamia said finally. "The baby looks great. Our testing all came back fine."

Everyone breathed a sigh of relief.

"We got approved for another year of housing, thanks to Jake," Sydney volunteered.

A general cheer filled the air.

"I told the landowner what I'd been doing," Cole said into the silence that followed. "He complimented me for my entrepreneurship and asked me to keep doing it once he upped the home insurance and looked into county permitting. I get to keep a portion of the funds for managing it."

Everyone looked at him, shocked.

"I know," Cole said, laughing. "Turns out he's not a bad billionaire."

Sadie felt intense relief. She'd been worried for Cole, and sweet Holly, and little Violet. Quite the turn of events for the billionaire to not be a bad guy, at least this once.

"Jerry and I are allowed to keep our businesses running," DeeDee said, and everyone cheered again.

"What a couple of weeks," Elaina said when the chatter had died down. They all sobered. "It won't get much better. Carl pled guilty to Royce's murder, but Preston's case is pending. The media will be asking us lots of questions. And the water isn't fixed. We're all in good health, thankfully, but a permanent solution will take time."

Everyone had gotten their test results back and aside from Jerry finding out he had high blood pressure and DeeDee having thyroid problems, it didn't appear anyone was suffering ill effects from the water contamination, at least so far. The Forest was still working on a solution, one they planned to bill Preston Chandler for. But the residents of Poplar had nowhere else to go, so they'd stick around until they figured it out.

"So, are we going to swim or what?" Karsen, the middle Cox kid, asked, and the grownups laughed.

"Go get changed, kids," Justin said, gesturing to the

changing rooms. Holly went in to change Violet, and the rest of them stood around.

"I don't think I can go in," DeeDee said finally.

Sadie shuddered. "Me either."

"Maybe this summer," Meadow said. "I just...I can't with all the steam, and the dark."

"It's super creepy," Megan said, and Travis and Sydney nodded.

"Maybe this will help," a voice said from behind them, and lights illuminated the pool deck. Twinkle lights had been strung across the fence, the changing rooms, and back and forth from the pitch of the changing hut to the rock slope. They changed the scene from creepy to warm.

Sadie turned, along with everyone else, to see Amos standing there. She smiled at him.

"Amos! You're back!"

"Yep," he said with a grin. "I'm rehired and cleared of wrongdoing." His eyes met Sadie's. "My Gran says thank you."

Sadie knew Lilith was thankful. She'd come by the bakery two days ago and placed orders for birthday cakes for all of her family members for the next year, her bracelets back and clanking happily. Sadie hoped that her debt to her table of regulars was repaid for now, and she wouldn't be subjected to more votes soon.

Then the roommates–ahem, the throuple–setup their Bluetooth speaker and pumped upbeat music through it, and DeeDee unpacked snacks from her backpack, and Elaina produced a thermos of mulled wine, and Jake unpacked thermoses of tea and cocoa. Suddenly, it was a party. Within a few minutes, everyone was in the pool save pregnant Tamia, who sat on the edge with her legs in, wrapped in a blanket and drinking cocoa. The three boys tossed a beach ball back and forth. Violet puttered around in her water wings, her pink fluffy hat threatening to fall down below her eyes. And Sadie wore her red bikini and clung to Jake, who held her firmly at his side.

She looked up at him.

"This isn't exactly how I saw this romantic evening at the hot springs going," she whispered in his ear.

"We'll have to come up another time, alone," he growled, nipping at the skin of her neck, and she giggled.

"Just promise me no dead bodies again, and I'm in," she said, and he laughed before capturing her mouth in a kiss.

The music and sounds of laughter filled the night, and murder was far from everyone's minds. The residents of Poplar had reclaimed their space, and Sadie felt comfortable sharing it with them.

# Chapter Thirty

The morning was cold, the coffee was hot, the line was long, and Moose's Bakery Hoback Junction was back open for business.

Sadie stood at the back of the kiosk near the door and watched the flurry of activity. She was superfluous to the operation now. Holly was the perfect manager, Travis was an excellent and charming barista who raked in the tips, and Mirabel had a knack for making drinks that quickly had customers asking for her specifically. Holly was interviewing additional baristas to pad out the schedule next week. Despite the setback of being closed after the vandalism, the kiosk was going to run in the black sooner than she'd expected. That was due to Kendall's work, and Sadie gave her all the credit.

"This one's for you, Sadie," Holly said, swinging away from the southbound window. Sadie ducked behind Travis at the sink and walked over to the door. She caught sight of a swoop of pink hair and peered down at Greg and Penny. Greg was driving, of course, and Penny leaned over from the passenger seat, her forest green velvet capelet falling open.

"Well hello you two," Sadie said.

"Hello," Greg said, his face breaking into a dopey grin.

Penny pressed a kiss into his shoulder and grinned up at Sadie. "We're headed in to Idaho Falls for shopping."

"And a hockey game," Greg added.

Sadie blinked at Penny. "Really?"

Penny nodded. "Yes. I told Greg I'd get into one sport for him. I like anything with a good fight, so we're trying hockey first." She pulled open her cape to reveal a worn Montana Magic Hockey t-shirt. "I even found this cute vintage tee at the thrift store!"

Greg looked down at her affectionately. "And I'm going to shop for some vintage clothes of my own. I think I could become a suspenders guy."

Sadie grinned at them. "That sounds like an excellent compromise. What kind of coffee can I get you for the trip? On me for saving my bacon last week. Thank you again, for that."

"And we'll do it again when we need to," Greg said, winking at her, and Sadie laughed. Like that was going to happen. She handed them their coffees, then waved goodbye, her heart warmed for her friend. Opposites did attract, especially when they were open to compromise.

"Switch ya again, Sadie," Holly said, laughing. "This side's demanding an audience with you."

Sadie sighed with fake irritation and whirled to that window to peer out.

She frowned when she saw Baxter's face. "I was expecting my handsome boyfriend," she complained.

"No dice, boss!" Sadie heard Kendall call from the backseat. "Come for a joyride with us!"

"But can we get coffee first?" Sully asked politely, if nasally, from the passenger seat.

"Sure," Sadie agreed. "I'm not needed here, anyway. I'll take a cinnamon swirl latte, Holly, and whatever these clowns want. Put it on my tab." She winked and turned to the backdoor to get her coat and purse, then exited through the back, the sound of Disney pop hits following her out. Holly couldn't quite get away from the kid tunes, even at work.

She got in on Kendall's side, and Kendall squeezed over next to Claire, who greeted Sadie enthusiastically.

Armed with coffees and cookies, they pulled away from the kiosk.

"Where are we going?" Sadie asked.

"You'll see," Kendall promised. The SUV turned north headed back to Jackson. The roads were clear, though snow was piled up everywhere. It had been a record-breaking winter so far, and it wasn't even February yet.

"How's Kamari doing?" Sadie took a sip of her latte. It was Holly's specialty, and her new favorite.

"She's riding a high like I've never seen," Kendall laughed. "She's filmed three days, and they asked her back for three more here, and then a few on location shoots."

"I'm so happy for her," Sadie grinned. "I can't wait to see her shredding it on the big screen."

"Next winter!"

"I'm going to miss her, though," Sadie frowned.

"I know, girl. But she'll still technically be my roommate, even if her hard ass never comes home." Kamari had formally put in her notice at the bakery, at least for the winter. She'd probably be back in the summer. A nice fat check from TGR meant she could go without income for a while.

"Time to hire more baristas," Sadie sighed.

"I'll help," Kendall said with a grin, and Sadie laughed.

"I'm sure you will."

They pulled into town and immediately turned left to head towards Wilson and Sadie looked around the car.

"Now do I get to know where we're going?"

"Still a surprise, Moose," Claire said.

But Sadie knew where they were going. And when Baxter pulled into the parking lot with easy on and off access from the highway, Sadie was already sold.

"Girl, you know I'm a yes on this," she said, looking at Kendall. "We need to get the business plan together and go to the bank for financing."

"Well..." Kendall said, her face pinking.

Claire cleared her throat. "I give better repayment options than a bank, Sadie. And I'm a completely silent partner when asked to be."

"Oh." Sadie swallowed hard. "Uh..."

"I didn't ask," Kendall said. "She offered."

"I did. Because I believe in both of you and your business. I'm not doing this because Kendall is my girlfriend. I'm doing this because I see an opportunity. Also, I'd like to get excellent coffee on my way to town in the mornings, and there's no easy drive-thru option here. So a little bit, this is for me."

"I'll need to see the contract," Sadie warned.

"Of course," Claire said. "You know how I feel about contracts."

"And we'll have to convince the owner of this building. What is it, anyway?"

Claire rolled her lips in. "I happen to own it."

"Since when?"

"Since...yesterday, when I bought it from the previous owner. It was an office building. It can be anything you want it to be, but for now it will be empty while you build the kiosk."

Sadie blinked at Claire. "Like...a secondary bakery location to ramp up the mail order and custom order business? And to supply the coffee kiosks to take the pressure off the main location?"

"That sounds reasonable. Note, there's also a second story that could be converted to housing."

"You're speaking my love language, Claire. Watch out. Remember, we were pretend married for an hour once."

Kendall puffed herself up. "Hands off my woman."

"What do you think, Sadie?" Claire asked, rolling her eyes.

Sadie took a deep breath. What was there to say, but yes? She felt like Cinderella, surprised by a fairy godmother. Except this fairy godmother was a billionaire with dubious mob connections and two henchmen. But Sadie liked her, and she knew she was a fair businesswoman with the right intentions for the valley. Plus, there would be contracts she would insist the lawyers look over very, very closely. This could be how all her dreams came true—an enlarged baking space, thriving satellite locations, more housing for employees. She couldn't say no.

"Of course I'm a yes," Sadie said, grinning. She felt tears at the corner of her eyes. "Of course I am."

"Yes!" Kendall punched the air, but hit the ceiling instead, wincing. "What if we named it...Nosy Bitch Coffee?"

Sadie snorted out a laugh and Claire punched Kendall in the shoulder while Baxter and Sully giggled in the front seat. "Not a chance," Sadie laughed. "At least not officially."

And then they were piling out of the car to hug and look in the building and walk around the parking lot, making plans. Kendall measured things with a tape measurer she had hooked on her Carhartts. Claire took pictures. Sadie dreamt. She couldn't wait to put this plan to paper, to run the numbers, to place the orders, to build, to see this dream to fruition. And she couldn't imagine better partners to work with. Sadie called Claire and Kendall over to take a selfie, but Baxter took her phone from her to get it right. He must have been well trained by Claire, because he took it up from hip height to get the best angle and snapped half a dozen, so she'd be happy with at least one.

Back in the car and headed into Jackson, Sadie posted it to her personal Instagram and tagged the two of them, grinning. She noticed a notification and pressed the button to bring it up. JH007 accepted your follow request.

Sadie stared at the notification, her heart beating fast. Her finger itched to click it, to see what information Merritt's profile might give her about his life, the information she'd wanted for so long. But she didn't click it. Instead, she swiped the notification to delete it and put her phone back in her pocket. She looked out the window. Beside her, Kendall and Claire were murmuring to each other. Sully and Baxter were arguing about a sportsball game. Her hunky boyfriend would get off work soon, and she'd slip down to his place to wake him up naughtily after his nap. She was a successful business owner, with a flagship store and soon two thriving coffee satellite shops, with the possibility of a third. She didn't need complications from a maybe-a-spy man that wanted to just drop in and out of her life. She had everything she needed. And after everything they'd been through, what else could possibly happen?

* * *

Thank you for reading! It means so much to me. If you liked this book, please leave a review on Amazon, Goodreads, or wherever you normally review books. Reviews help indie authors like me get new readers!

What happens next? Sadie and the gang appear next in my Valentine's Day short story, A DEADLY SECRET ADMIRER, available for FREE at www.suepepperauthor.com/books

The Jackson Hole Moose's Bakery Not So Cozy Mystery Series continues in BOSS BABE MURDER, available in print wherever books are sold and in ebook on Amazon and Kindle Unlimited on 4/26/22!

# Author's Note

My family spent three winters in Jackson Hole, cozied up in our small wood-stove-heated house in employee housing. Maybe it's the haze of nostalgia, but even remembering the endless snow removal and wood hauling chores and the power and internet outages and the sheer terror of waking up to the sound of a slab of snow sliding off our metal roof in the night, I still would go back in a minute. The community, the snow globe feel of every day, the crackling wood stove and steaming mug of tea...it's what hygge dreams are made of.

Pritchard Hot Springs are a product of my imagination, but they're inspired by the very real Granite Hot Springs, which sit at the end of a mountain road maintained by a Forest Service groomer in the winter, accessible only by snowmobile, cross-country ski, or sled dogs. They're about an hour or so from Jackson, and many outfitters run winter trips. In the summer, you can drive there, and even camp if you're early enough to snag a spot. Astoria Hot Springs, where our story culminates, is real, and reopened to much fanfare in Summer 2020, one bright spot of that year. Both are very much worth a visit.

Much to my eternal consternation, there is no drive through

coffee kiosk in Hoback Junction, Wyoming. If someone local with the funds to make it happen is reading this, please go make the money. It's there. Everyone who drives through wants coffee. PLEASE MAKE THIS HAPPEN. All I ask is that you name the kiosk after me. Or Moose's. Or Tyrone.

The water quality issues at the heart of this mystery are very real. You can find out more about Hoback Junction's crisis, and what faces Jackson Hole at www.jhcleanwater.org.

As discussed in each Moose's Bakery mystery, Jackson is in the midst of a housing crisis. Many, many people, including my family, have been forced out of the community because of income inequality, a lack of affordable housing, and encroaching billionaires. I am donating a portion of the profits from this series to ShelterJH, an organization building grassroots and political power in Jackson Hole so that all community members can live where they work. I encourage you to give them your support and read through their policy platform. They have much better ideas on how to fix the problem than my works of fiction provide.

# Acknowledgments

I am grateful, as always, to my family and friends for their support, particularly Whitney, Rachael, Kristen, and Leah. Y'all get me through the days.

Thank you to my great friend and beta reader, Lea. I have a folder called "Lea's Ideas" and I will get to all of them, promise.

Thank you to my Advanced Reader team—you help get this book into the hands of more readers because of your thoughtful early reviews, and I appreciate you so much!

Thank you to my Sisters in Crime Guppy Chapter critique group partners. And thanks always for the support of my home chapter, Sisters in Crime Columbia River.

To our former Jackson Hole neighbors—I promise I only used your positive traits as inspiration when writing this and the negative ones were totally figments of my imagination. You know we'd be back in a minute if we could.

My husband fielded even more questions than normal on this book and was also an enthusiastic early reader. Thanks for reading this book in bed next to me and laughing appropriately at all the jokes. You know when you walk around the house in long johns after a cold outside day and you pull them up to your knees and your shins show? That's super sexy. Keep doing it.

Dear children, I love you. Thanks for the snuggles and the laughs and for putting up with mama locking herself in the bedroom to write. Everything I do, I do for you.

# About the Author

Sue Pepper writes not so cozy mysteries in the Pacific Northwest where she lives with her two kids, fuzzy yellow dog, and real life action hero husband. A former resident of Jackson Hole pushed out by the billionaire-caused housing crisis, she enjoys writing revenge and redemption for the fictional residents of her Jackson Hole Moose's Bakery Not So Cozy Mystery series, starting with her debut, Mountain Town Murder.

facebook.com/suepepperauthor

twitter.com/suepepperauthor

instagram.com/suepepperauthor

tiktok.com/@suepepper

# Also by Sue Pepper

**Jackson Hole Moose's Bakery Not So Cozy Mystery Series**

Available in print wherever books are sold, and in ebook form on Amazon and Kindle Unlimited:

Mountain Town Murder, #1

Hot Springs Murder, #2

Boss Babe Murder, #3 (4/26/22)

FREE interstitial short stories available at www.suepepperauthor.com/books:

Escape From the North Pole, #1.5

A Deadly Secret Admirer, #2.5

www.ingramcontent.com/pod-product-compliance
Lightning Source LLC
Chambersburg PA
CBHW020152310726
48970CB00006B/2110